Buffalo Chief

JANE & PAUL
ANNIXTER

Buffalo Chief

HOLIDAY HOUSE — NEW YORK

TO

STANLEY VESTAL

WITH HEARTY APPRECIATION

Table of Contents

Buffalo Chief

CHAPTER ONE
Kahtanka

FOLLOWING the northward trail of the great buffalo herd, a band of Oglala Sioux was camped at a
bend of the Powder River. On the sparsely wooded
bank were nearly a hundred conical, smoke-brown
tipis, their cones of many poles like tilted war lances.
Only last night had the Indians come, yet dawn
found them as well ordered and established as if
they had lived here for many months, each lodge and
family in its own relative position in its customary
circle of tipis. Most prominent was the tall tipi of
Chief Horned Thunder, painted yellow. Beside it, as
always, was the lodge of Standing Elk, *shaman* or
tribal oracle of the Oglala.

11

It was early morning, but already the camp was full of activity. The old men sat gravely warming themselves in the first sunlight, while the squaws cooked *wasna* in the outdoor kitchens of green boughs. This was a mixture of ground buffalo meat, marrow, and the first spring berries, which the children were bringing in. Some of the young men moved here and there on guard, or tended the ponies that were picketed at the edge of the village. Others were making preparations for a game dance, for the spring buffalo hunt would soon be on. Meat must be put by, pemmican made, hides taken for the making of bull-boats, bow thongs, tipis, drums, and moccasins, and horns shaped into cups, spoons and ceremonial head gear.

As always before a game dance, Standing Elk had withdrawn to his lodge to smoke, sing and make mystery. The *shaman* was famed as a far-seer and dream-teller and credited with the power of "bringing buffalo." Also he was said to have the power to pacify the buffalo spirit and hold the animals from flight.

While he chanted and prayed the ceremonial drums began to throb. Usually Standing Elk sang among the elders, but of late he had had dark forebodings, and today felt a need to commune directly with the herd spirit. So, as the two rows of dancers faced each other, representing the hunters and the hunted, and the chant of propitiation rose, Standing Elk went for his horse, tethered by the stream.

As he mounted, he was aware of Hawk, his thirteen-year-old son, beside him, looking up.

"May I go with you, my father?"

Standing Elk gave a sign of assent. It pleased him that the boy should leave the excitement of the ceremonial to follow him; for he knew how the talk of the young hunters fired Hawk's blood. The boy's blood was already half fire, Standing Elk was wont to think. It was this quality which had given Hawk his name, for once the hawk has begun his diving descent, his stoop, nothing can stop him nor can he stop himself. Nevertheless it had long been the *shaman's* secret hope that Hawk would follow in his own footsteps on the medicine path. Standing Elk was no longer young and the mantle of his calling and the wisdom of a lifetime must soon be passed on to another.

Following the recent tracks of the bison, father and son rode up-country until from the top of a rise they could look down upon the vast herd spread out for miles over the plain and hills, even filling the coulee bottoms like dark rivers. This was part of the great Continental Herd, thousands upon thousands moving eastward and northward now after wintering on the South Dakota plains. It was indeed a great herd still, but not so great as even a snow or two ago, the *shaman* reflected. In his memory the bison had been numberless as the leaves on the trees, at times covering a hundred miles of game plains like one vast robe, the totem and the cattle of the Sioux, the tribe's wealth and its security. It was not the plague or any Indian hunting that was responsible for this fall-off in numbers; it was the growing army of white hunters on the plains to the south. No matter how ample the spring calving, it could not make up for such losses.

The *shaman* let his thoughts down to the deep place in the breast where a real thing may be known. Still within and still without, he sent his spirit forth to become one with the spirit of the herd. He spoke in the solemn manner of the ancient ceremonies which went back to a far time when men and animals communed as one:

"They will be coming soon, the young men. Some of you will die that we may live. But you must forgive, for our people are hungry and offerings will be made to Wahkan-Tanka, the giver of all."

The *shaman* began to chant now, half-hoping to hear Hawk's voice join in, but the boy was gone when he glanced around. Never still for long, that one. Seldom there when you looked again. Where was he now?

Standing Elk was moving on over the rise when he heard the bawl of a buffalo cow in labor and saw several cows gathering in a hollow just below him. They were waiting in stillness for some event and the *shaman* knew what this must be. He, too, waited and presently witnessed the birth, his heart warming as he saw the new-born struggling up on stiff legs. Often an hour and more passed before a new calf even attempted to rise, but this one was soon standing. A strong one, a brave one, this, already knowing his own and his way, for now he had reached his mother and was being licked clean as he stood staggering and bunting beneath her, seeking his first meal.

Almost black, he was, like the great chief bulls, and as he watched Standing Elk was taken by a vision. Here at his very beginning was a grandfather one among buffalo, destined to lead and to sacrifice, like all great chiefs, for his people. Yet Standing Elk was sensing death, too. In his head he was hearing the buffalo *pahaiyaane,* The-Noise-When-Nothing-Is-About. This was a sound to be heard only when something needs to be known. It came from the spirit herd which moved with the living one and forever called to it.

Standing Elk could not tell all that should be known, but a sense of dread filled him, a fear for his own people, and for the great herd. A time of change was beginning and he felt that there was great need for this black calf to live. This need brought from the *shaman* a chant, invoking protection that would be like a ring-pass-not around the little bull. Kahtanka, he named him, Chief Bull.

As suddenly as he had gone and as silently, Hawk was beside Standing Elk once more. The *shaman* did not ask the boy where he had been, but continued to watch the new calf in the midst of the concerned and motherly cows.

"The new-born has a mark like a white star on his forehead, my father," said Hawk.

"Your eyes are sharp, my son!" Standing Elk replied. "That is a special sign, a mark of powerful medicine. Truly this is one of the master bulls. Do not speak of this thing, my son," he added, "or the power may leave."

They turned their horses quietly toward camp. Wind-Old-Woman was sweeping down from the Bighorn Peaks. By late afternoon it would be cutting and cruel as a squaw with a scalping knife, but Kahtanka would be sheltered well, Standing Elk knew.

The ceremony of the game chant was over now, and there would be only normal activities in camp until the buffalo hunt started. In their lodge opening Standing Elk's wife, Willow Woman, was scraping a stretched deerhide, singing softly at her work. The *shaman's* daughter, Wood Mouse, was busy nearby, softening a skin for moccasins. Wood Mouse was older than Hawk, and already young men came to sing outside the lodge in the early dark.

As Hawk took the two horses to picket in a nearby meadow, the *shaman* went into his lodge to smoke and ponder and draw out the full meaning of what he had seen. Once more he breathed the words of the protective ring-pass-not about the small black one.

"*Wahkan-Tanka!*" The name of the Great Mysterious, the Buffalo God of the Sioux, came from his lips. *Wahkan-Tanka*, who sometimes walked abroad in the form of a great buffalo bull and spoke to men. Truly the spirit was close at hand today.

A S   T H E luminous, star-studded darkness came over the plain that night the new calf shivered beneath his mother, for all that he stood strongly upright and did not lean against her legs. It was not only the cold cutting through his tender skin that made him shiver, it was what was out there in the dark, strange and fearsome. Low forms flitted in and out. At times they swept in close enough to be smelled and seen. There were green-lit eyes, whole clusters of them. Kahtanka was terribly tired and wanted to lie down, but he dared not, he must keep moving with his mother. Now there was a snarl and a snapping of jaws only a few feet away, and the carrion breath was like death itself. His mother wheeled and wheeled with lowered head, sparring agilely with ready horns. She was old in this warfare and with her new calf to protect her strength and speed were doubled.

The coyotes flung back upon themselves like a wave but were in again at another angle with a wild hysterical yapping designed to frighten game to rout. They knew that soon the tired calf must settle down, a tender lump upon the ground, never so delectable as on this first night. But the mother's bawling cries brought other cows and the coyote cordon looped back into thicker darkness. Their baffled wailing was cut through with blood-thirsty yips and challenges as they waited for another chance.

The three protecting cows that surrounded the black calf were nudging both him and his mother deeper into the herd. At last Kahtanka felt warm and safe and dropped off where he stood. But presently he awoke, all asprawl on the ground, to the anxious bunting of his mother's muzzle. Now the real enemy of the night had found them out. The calf struggled up, trembling anew at what he saw and smelled: four gaunt, phosphor-eyed forms were gliding toward him, lean and high in the shoulder, their backs sloping downward to low hind quarters and bush tails. Buffalo wolves, these were, inches higher than the ordinary gray or timber wolf, and capable of pulling down a grown buffalo when working together. The bison ranks milled about in fear as those four threaded the mass toward the new black calf.

Swiftly a ring of cows formed a protective circle of lowered heads around the calf. Their defiant bellows brought one of the guardian bulls pounding up in a wrathful charge that quickly scattered the killers. This was Kahtanka's own father, one of the four great master bulls of the herd, as much bigger than an ordinary bull buffalo as a grizzly is bigger than a

black bear. He stormed back and forth, charging the
wolves again and again with tossing horns, his bellows of anger shaking the very ground. Agile as they
were, the wolves barely escaped the side-swipes of
that vast horned head, grown crafty from countless
battles. At some signal from the leader the wolves
melted into the darkness to seek a safer banquet.

Thereafter the big bull stayed near, looming vast
as a prairie hillock to the eyes of the calf, darker than
the night itself and giving off an aura of safety. The
calf slept then for hours, his mother also.

Dawn was like another life without fear. The calf
felt rested and strong, strong enough to bunt and
heave with his forehead as he fed. All about him,
over the closely bunched herd, hung a steamy vapor.
The young calves leapt and frolicked. The buffalo
birds that perched each night along the spines of the
big old bulls busied themselves searching out para-
sites in the matted wool of their great hosts. These
cowbirds were rusty brown members of the black-
bird family, and there were hundreds of them peck-
ing and calling this morning, above the shaggy army
of the herd.

Warm as well as safe and sated, Kahtanka followed his mother to the river. When she waded into

the stream he bawled from the bank. Afterward, drying in the sun, she combed and dressed his soft new mane again and again with her deft black tongue. He reveled in the warmth. In this bright, new-green world studded with crocuses, even the memory of the night terrors was quite erased.

As the morning advanced, the interrelated family groups that made up the big herd drew off by themselves. These were mostly in charge of weathered old cows, grandmothers and great-grandmothers of their clan who had much to do with the actual government of the herd. Younger cows and calves followed them. Round about, in dry coulee bottoms, clouds of dust rose, pawed up by restless young bulls, who were shunted off by themselves at the age of two. At times there were sounds like falling rock heard from a distance as a pair of three-year-olds tried out their strength, crashing their horned heads together, shoving and roaring like lions until one of the pair found himself hung on the other's horns—to be quickly released, for all this was spring play, with the rutting season still many months distant.

Down closer to the river other bulls knelt to gore up the earth, to turn round and round to deepen their holes and make a wallow for themselves. The best natural wallows as well as the best shade were preempted by the big leading bulls, each having his own chosen place respected by all wherever the herd stopped, season after season. Toward midday all who could reach the muddy shallows covered their almost hairless hind quarters with wet clay against the sting of deer flies which were a plague even this early in the spring. Afterwards they would climb the river bank to stand and bake in the noonday sun.

Up on his chosen rise of ground stood the great bull who was Kahtanka's father, apparently asleep, but watchfully alert as he overlooked the herd, while the cowbirds rose from the slope of his back and settled again. Once when anger got the better of two young bulls the herd master moved down-slope, abruptly looming over them and shouldering them apart. Then he returned to his stand on the hillock, facing again into the north and east, as if waiting for some message out of the air, the impulse to move, perhaps. Calving time was over now and the greening buffalo grass was covering the land. All that afternoon gaggles of wild geese and tattered wedges of ducks swept over toward the north, verifying the fact that spring had come to the farthest limits of the buffalo range. Growing in the big bull was the lure of the lush pastures of the north. Movement of the bison along their time-worn trails to the north and east was almost due again, something as inevitable as the movement of the planets.

The high signal calls of coyotes told of another night approaching. The wailing cries brought back the memory of fear to the black calf, all the cold and terror he had forgotten in the bright sunlight. The first part of this night was like the one before it, except that the calf was more agile and more alert. He and his mother moved together into the thick of the herd and the skirmish attacks of wolves and coyotes were but sounds in the distance.

Then the deep night brought a different kind of killer, slow but fearless, and relying on neither speed nor bluff.

Two bears had come down from the distant mountains following the appetizing scent of buffalo. With no sound beyond a lustful grunt or two they moved in on the herd and made a quick kill. Phlegmatic and nerveless, the pair fell to feeding at once. The ranks of buffalo in the vicinity swirled in upon themselves wild-eyed, and to the black calf came the new composite fear-smell of blood and bear. He started a small stampede all his own until his moth-

er blocked his way. Then one of the younger guardian bulls attacked the killers and there were sounds
of tearing and crunching and bawls of defiance and
challenge all blent in a wild confusion.

The bull would have routed a single bear in a
matter of minutes, but a bear in front and another
behind made a terrible fighting machine. The self-
elected guardian was being bashed in the neck and
head and ridden down from behind at the same
time. He sent up a bellow for help that brought the
old leader himself surging through the ranks.

A deft side-sweep of the vast head and the bear
on the back of the young bull sailed momentarily
against the star-shine. He alighted all asprawl and
before he could gain his feet twenty-five hundred
pounds of avenging bison loomed over him with
goring horns and pounding hoofs. The bear was
flattened into a shapeless and bloody pelt upon the
ground. The other bear tried to box and dodge but
was outsparred by black horns and took a hasty de-
parture.

Again morning brought forgetfulness, brightness
and warmth to the new-born bull calf. This day
there were no drawn-out lollings in the sun and ev-
en when they went down to the stream there was no

dallying. Kahtanka's mother drank methodically, then nosed him into the water, too. It was so clear that it looked as far away as the sky and the calf's whole head went under before he knew it. He came up blowing and swallowing, having had enough water for a long time.

His mother and his many aunts seemed watchful and restless as they cropped the bunchgrass. Few of the bison lay down that morning or rolled in the wallows. On knoll after knoll bulls could be seen standing, heads into the wind. Even the cowbirds seemed to be watching and waiting. They wheeled and called above the backs of the buffalo as a restless stirring swept over the thousands. It permeated the mass like the first heave of troubled waters at the approach of a storm. All now were catching the luring memory of the north and were ready to move, only awaiting the signal from the master bulls. Each time one of these mounted a hillock the lesser bulls moved watchfully closer and the surrounding herd paused in its sketchy feeding.

Yet another night found them where they were. That night Kahtanka expected disturbances, for the waves of fear that told of the killers on the fringes of the herd were already familiar to him. He reacted more or less automatically with those around him and willingly followed his mother into the safety of the center of the herd.

The next morning there was a new and different menace. Somewhere in the herd, not far distant, he sensed terror, heard bellowings and high strange cries of creatures Kahtanka knew nothing about. There were sudden roars of sound, growing pressure in and around him, and a far rumble of many hoofs that meant stampede. The thunder and the heat of it rolled in upon them all, stirring them to erratic flight. For the first time his mother, too, was in complete rout and it was only Kahtanka's extra edge of strength and nimbleness which kept him from going under the pounding hoofs. As he was swept along beneath and beside her the wild high cries he heard were like the coyote pack and in the hot dark shadow of the many close-pressed bodies it seemed to him like night again.

Abruptly then their flight had carried them into a calmer area of the herd. He saw that it was truly day and that it was no coyote pack that had attacked them but another sort of killer, one that Kahtanka was to know much more about.

CHAPTER TWO

First Kill

THOUGH HE had not known for sure that he would be using them soon, Hawk had been making arrows for the past two moons. Not the small, blunt arrows which boys used to shoot at birds and squirrels, but flint-headed arrows, ground sharp as knives. He had modeled them carefully after the arrows of Dead-Come-Back-Man, one of the elders of the Oglala who had been a great warrior in his time. Dead-Come-Back-Man had also helped Hawk shape and string a man-size bow, telling him the while the tale of his own first hunt when he had won the name of Panther Boy.

It was as he had looked down at the great buffalo

herd with his father that it suddenly came to Hawk that he could wait no longer to prove himself. He must join in the coming hunt. He had the bow and the arrows in the lodge of Dead-Come-Back-Man, who had kept his secret well. What he did not have yet was a grown man's strength. But he had the will.

At dawn on the morning of the hunt Hawk slipped away to the tipi of Dead-Come-Back-Man. His old friend was already up and sitting by his small fire. Hawk knew where his bow and arrows were kept wrapped in a piece of deerskin and went to the place without words. Dead-Come-Back-Man was watching him. Meeting the boy's eye, he held it long and in silence across the fire.

"I must!" Hawk said, answering the look. "The time has come."

"Then I have nothing to say," the elder told him. "The time is for the hunter himself to know."

It was his father's fastest horse that Hawk sought out, a piebald with four white feet. Then he rode to the top of a hill to watch for the start of the hunt. Waiting, he thought only of what he intended to do and how the thing might be done.

At last the party of twenty-one young hunters

came in sight, riding fast and in close formation. Hawk saw that Hurries-To-War was in the lead as usual, and behind him young South Bear, a fire-eat-er with many war *coups* to his credit. There were but three old muzzle-loading rifles in the party, all the other hunters carrying bows and arrows. Hawk let them get well ahead, then followed at a fast lope, his deerskin shirt-tails flying and flapping as he cut a circle to the side.

The party was nearing the buffalo herd before Hawk was noticed. Seeing his big bow, the hunters called out jeering shouts of *"On-hey!"* to quell and shame the boy beyond following. *"On-hey!"* was the shout a warrior gave when he struck or touched an enemy to count *coup* in battle. Ignoring the mock-ery, Hawk followed on, sometimes at a tangent, but always circling in again. Soon the hunters were watching him in silence, no longer merely amused and mocking.

Hawk felt keenly their new seriousness. They would not drive him off, he knew; it was not the Sioux way to stop even a boy bent on a feat of cour-age or name-hunting. But neither would they help or advise him, or make allowance for his youth and in-experience. It was a bold step he had taken, throwing off the protection as well as the fetters of youth. If he was injured it was his own concern. If he failed he would be shamed and laughed at. Better to be killed than that!

He veered aside, asking no quarter.

Hawk was the first to reach the game. He did not stop at the fringe of the herd but lanced his mount into the thick of the mass as he had seen the boldest hunters do. Before him and on both sides buffalo milled and churned uneasily. Behind him he heard shots and the high wild yelling of the young men. The milling buffalo broke into thundering flight and he was carried along in the surging brown tide.

Hawk's horse, though trained as a buffalo runner, was almost out of hand with fear, here in the midst of the herd. No escape except straight up, which was what the piebald was trying for, white-eyed and snorting in panic. Hawk clung to the mane, leaning far forward. Stumble of horse or slip of rider would be fatal here; the fallen one would be ground to pulp within a minute. Even if he would, Hawk could not have used his bow now. It took all he had just to stay with his horse. Nor was there space on either side to drive an arrow home. The thick rising heat of the many huge bodies enveloped him, blent with the musky smell of animal flesh and fur so overpowering that he drowned in it for a time.

When Hawk's consciousness broke through the darkness it seemed that the earth was tipping and there were buffalo swinging in the sky. A deep, dull reverberation filled all the air, the thunder of countless hoofs. Leaning far forward along his horse's neck and mane, he spoke quiet words into its brown ear until by slow degrees the snorting of fear and the plunging eased.

On they swept, sometimes with space about them now, but they could not have gotten out of the crush or stopped had they tried. Hawk waited for another shifting in the mass, then chose his kill, a young bull off to his right. Gradually he kneed his mount closer, jerked an arrow from his quiver and snapped it to the string. With all his strength he bent the bow, drawing the arrow back to its flint head.

Thwack! The feathered shaft sank half its length behind the shoulder, a bit too high for the heart. The rush of the young bull never slackened. Hawk rushed after him, as if tied to his quarry by a thong. He fitted another arrow to the bow. This time as he came abreast of his game he reached far under the horse's neck with his left arm, clinging with his right leg and right arm, his left leg far down under the belly of his horse. He let go a second shaft inches below the first. The young buffalo bellowed yet pounded on, big head low, liquid eyes gleaming wildly beneath the curled and matted fur.

Scalding shame poured through Hawk. He was not strong enough to bring down game, even with a man-sized bow and perfect arrows! The hunters would laugh and mock him, for no doubt they had seen. Even the girls would hear of it and titter as he passed.

The side of the young bull was dripping red, the eyes rolling whitely now in panic and pain. This animal would suffer much, for it would be hours or days from now before he would die.

Suddenly Hawk knew that he could not let the young buffalo go. He had marked it for his own. He must bring it down even if he had to follow it on into the country of the Crows to the west. He reached back for another arrow, then sudden fury made him fling his bow aside. He whipped the quiver up over his head and threw it away. Now Hawk waited his chance and drove his mount in so close that his knee was pressing the wounded bull's flank. He jerked up his legs so that for an instant he was crouched on all fours on the bare back of his galloping pony, then launched himself outward and fastened with clutching hands to the fur of the buffalo's hump. With a wild whinny his horse veered crazily off and Hawk was left there literally riding his prey.

In spite of clutching hands and clamped legs he did not know whether he could hang to the pain-crazed bull or not. His buffalo mount was crashing now through low brush and Hawk's legs and sides were cut with whipping branches till the blood ran. There was no give to that wide, rock-hard back, no let-up in the buffalo's pounding gait. The stiff short legs seemed jointless, springless and the hoofs came down like ungiving stone. Hawk felt the spasms of terror that tore through the animal and it took all his remaining strength to crawl slowly forward onto the sloping neck. It was slightly softer there, but lying out as he was his head was lower than his body, for the head of the buffalo all but swept the ground. He offered up swift prayer to sun and moon and called upon the earth spirit, who presided over all man's hunting. Then his knife was in his right hand and, risking death again, he reached far down to stab and stab beneath the bull's straining neck. The animal's blood spurted, covering Hawk's arm. Still the young bull pounded on and would not die.

Leaning close to one stiff black ear, Hawk voiced the ceremonial words of the buffalo-hunter: "Grandfather, my people are hungry. You were created for this, so I must kill you." On his own he added: "Grandfather, fight and run no longer. You are very tired!"

Even so it seemed an endless time before the animal's gait began to falter. Then suddenly the downthrust head and horns gored the earth, and Hawk was flung forward and free of the crashing fall. Instantly he was on all fours, scuttling back to lie in the lee of the now prone body of his kill while hundreds of buffalo coming from behind barely broke their ranks around the fallen one and the small figure huddled behind it.

For an endless time humped forms continued to hurtle past in a wild confusion of pounding hoofs, rolling eyes and froth-strung muzzles. There was an end at last. But even then Hawk stayed low, offering up his thanks to *Wahkan-Tanka*, the Great One, for this miracle.

WHEN THE first of the hunters arrived, Hawk was too busy even to look up. Red-armed, he had already taken the tongue and heart of his kill, and with the skill of a seasoned hunter had slit the hide down the belly and girdled the four legs.

"I, Hawk, have killed this one!" was all he said.

But more than that was on record, for through a break in the ranks of the herd both South Bear and Eagle Seizer had glimpsed the end of Hawk's ride and the final knifing. Very different the hunters' smiles were now. One man sighted Hawk's pony circling afar and rode out and brought it in.

Indicating the sixty dead buffalo strewn over a mile of plain, Hurries-To-War said, "We are going back to bring the women for the skinning-out. You had better ride with us."

Hawk answered firmly, "I, Hawk, will skin this one out!"

Darkness had almost fallen when Hawk rode into camp with the hide, heart and tongue of his kill, his bare legs and arms blood-encrusted. He was bone-weary but content, for the story of his triumph had gone before him through the camp so that there was awe in the eyes of his playmates who had run out to meet him. Trills and sighs came from the girls and young women as Hawk rode in among the tall tipis.

Standing Elk came and took hold of Hawk's thong bridle, calling out as was the custom.

"Look, my son has become a hunter! My son is brave!"

Horned Thunder, the war chief, was standing near. A smile broke through his fierce owl visage as he said, "It is but a little way from a fearless hunter to the brave warrior."

Now Standing Elk led Hawk, still riding the piebald, round the great circle of lodges for all to see. Hawk had to hold hard to hide his feelings, yet he accepted the honor proudly, for his courage was too real a thing to admit a false modesty.

THAT NIGHT there was feasting in the Sioux camp and the dance of thanksgiving that followed a successful hunt. In the tipi of Standing Elk, around the small fire, visitors came and went. Hawk was asked and re-asked to tell the story of his hunt. He related it all simply and gravely. Across the fire the eyes of Willow Woman and Wood Mouse gleamed with pride and pleasure. To show his appreciation of the honor to his son, Standing Elk gave away a horse to

an elder who had recently lost his. To Hawk he gave
the piebald pony. It was the father's privilege to give
his boy a new name, had he wished, but Standing
Elk decided against it. Hawk was a fine name and
there was none he could think of that fitted the boy
so well.

Truly he was proud of his son and thankful to
Wahkan-Tanka for watching over the boy on this
eventful day. But the *shaman* realized that his own
unvoiced wish had fallen earthward, as indeed he
had feared it might. For today, it was plain, Hawk
had chosen his own course. He would go swiftly
along it and far, but it would be the warrior's path,
not the *shaman's* own. Standing Elk knew that in
the years to come his people would need the vision
of a true *shaman* as much as they needed a great
chief. And who would it be? Sun Dreamer of the
Hunkpapa, greatest of them all, had been gone these
many years. Looks-To-An-Owl, the Sans Arc medicine man, was a fake, swaying the people by fear,
with a creature of darkness for his totem. Looks-To-
An-Owl had none of the powers of the true dream-
teller and far-seer, such as he himself possessed, nor
the great heart of the true chief or *shaman*. True,
Sitting Bull, oracle of the Hunkpapa, had all of these

things. For the present Standing Elk must put his hope in him.

Having done his duty according to custom, Standing Elk left the fire-lit circle and sought the lodge of his chief. He stood coughing politely outside the opening of Horned Thunder's tipi until the voice of the chief bade him enter. Horned Thunder sat by his small fire with Eagle Seizer, a seasoned warrior, and White Antelope, sub-chief of the Oglala. The war chief's wife and another squaw sat in the far shadows.

"Sit and smoke with us, Grandfather," said Horned Thunder, addressing the *shaman* by the term of greatest respect. "You should be happy tonight," he added. "You have a brave son in your lodge."

The *shaman* smiled. "One sets out to raise owls and finds a young falcon in the nest."

"Truly, it is a time to raise falcons," the chief said. "When the Blue Coats fall upon a peaceful village and kill all, even the women and children—you know this black thing happened but five moons ago at Sand Creek—it is time for all Sioux to become falcons and eagles! It is a bloody time on the plains, for the white man is bent on our destruction and we must fight for our lives. Has not Sitting Bull of the

Hunkpapa asked us to unite against the enemy?"

"Only today smoke signals on the hills told of more Blue Coats coming toward the Powder," said Eagle Seizer.

Standing Elk spoke: "And all the time the white men have been talking peace and making treaties with us, they have been fighting a war among themselves! Now, it is said, the Great White Father himself at Washington has been killed, shot dead by one of his own people."

"I have heard this thing," said Horned Thunder. "How can we trust a people who cannot trust themselves!"

"While they bring war to us," observed Standing Elk, "they bring great death to the buffalo. Which is worse?"

"We, the Sioux, can fight back. The buffalo are helpless," White Antelope pointed out.

While all were silent in full recognition of this, Standing Elk felt that the moment had come to speak of what had brought him here.

"My vision of three days ago has returned and completed itself," he said.

"We are listening." Horned Thunder inclined his head respectfully.

"The great herd, already dwindled, will shrink rapidly until it is a great herd no longer! The buffalo is our totem. As they go, we go. Already there is a shadow herd of the dead with every living herd and the shadow herd is greater."

"*Hau!* I have seen such a herd in my dreams!" said the chief.

"No dream," the *shaman* said, "but a real thing. The shadow herd is there calling to the other and the living herd is answering. Death is in the air."

White Antelope spoke quietly: "Death comes, much death, but the spring always brings more buffalo, new calves."

"The spring calving can no longer make up for the killing," Standing Elk said. "You in your time, and perhaps I in mine, will see the end of all! Both the herds and the tribes are in great danger. All our chiefs know this; all fear for the future. No medicine can change this now."

The chief smoked for a time in silence, for the breath of dark portent seemed to have passed through the lodge. Finally he spoke.

"It is a time for wise leadership. We who are responsible for the good of the people must work together."

Standing Elk nodded. "One prays for this. Also that there will be wise chiefs among the buffalo for the bad time ahead."

Now the *shaman* rose, raised his hand in a gesture of peace, and left the lodge.

CHAPTER THREE

Beaverskin

TWO WEEKS had passed and the herd had come to rest again on the Little Missouri, sixty miles north and east. The spring movement north was always slow because of the many new calves. Once more the herd master stood on the crest of a hill, head low. The wind fingered his shaggy black-brown beard and frontlet which just swept the ground. Now and again the eyes of the resting buffalo roundabout turned to him as they fed or drowsed. All day many heads had been lifting, dozens of eyes focusing on his every movement as he stood his post. After a time he dropped to his knees, lowered his great body and bedded down on the crest. But he did not sleep.

42

Naturally short-sighted and with hearing that was none too good, the bison relied chiefly on their phenomenal sense of smell for protection. Later, when the wind shifted, the old leader was aware of a fox's den fully a mile away; also of a prairie-dog village beyond the distant bend of the river. There was scent, too, of another village even farther away, the spring camp of the Minniconjou Sioux, moving westward to take their toll of the big herd. Soon their hunters would be coming, sweeping into the bison ranks on fast horses to kill as the Oglala had done, and after them the other tribes along the buffalo trails, well known for ages past. This was an inevitable part of the herd's migration, to be expected and accepted, like the nightly attacks of wolf and coyote, or cruel turns in the weather. The leader knew all this. Why did he not move the herd northward at once? It was as if the bison had a tryst with all these killers, and must await them in turn, at times even hastening to meet them.

It was afternoon when the leader sensed that human hunters were coming. He was standing now. He had heard nothing, seen nothing; it was an indefinable warning impressed by none of the five senses but an overtone of all of them. Because he

was their leader he was given this synthetic percep-
tion and, being leader, he could not share with them
the extra minutes of unsuspecting peace before the
first actual sounds of the Indians' approach could
be heard.

As leader, also, he must now cut short this peace
of the herd. He gave a low, subterranean bellow
which sent his four buffalo-birds into the air and
brought the eyes of the younger bulls and several
weathered old cows round to him. The alert ran
through the ranks. A shifting and swirling took place
as in a stirred bowl, cows and young folding in toward the center of the herd, bulls to the outer edge.

Now on a slope to the north of them, though beyond their short-range vision, a band of wild mus-
tangs broke into sudden flight. Still it was long before the lonely landscape gave other sign. Then out
from the shadow of a butte rode a single file of Minniconjou hunters, soundless and circumspect as a
line of scouting coyotes, whose tactics they had imi-
tated for hundreds of years. The buffalo showed no
undue fear until, with a yelping signal, the leading
brave sliced his horse in toward the herd.

There were no rifles among these hunters and the
silent kills with bow and arrow caused little or no

stampeding in the herd. The main fear came from
the death cries of the stricken and the smell of blood
that brought as always a concerted treble bawling
from the shifting mass, a sound imbued with name-
less terror and a hopeless fate. This scent the bison
would fear to the end, yet it was so old and deep in
them that it was somehow tolerable. As before, Kahtanka panicked at the first impact of the blood-death
smell, but as his mother and the other cows roundabout grew quiet, he, too, shed his fear and began
batting his knobbly forehead against that of a brown
calf his own age.

In less than half an hour the killing was over and
the herd moved afar from its dead. Long before the
hunters had skinned out their kills the bison were
feeding again, a mile or two away. Now they were
ready to move on again, as if their spring mission
here were completed. With the early summer, particularly in the north and east, they were less and
less liable to encounter human hunters.

Before sunset came the leader's signal to move.
Through the northward cuts and valleys buffalo
flowed like a dark sluggish flood and the reverberation of their countless hoofs echoed far away like
thunder. Now came one of the few times when the

herd master could relax and rest after a fashion, for once they were in motion along the immemorial trails, habit itself took over in his place.

By now the spring calves were able to keep pace. This leg of the journey was far faster than the first, and in ten full hours it scarcely varied from its peculiar travel gait, neither trot nor gallop, but a sort of rocking lope. A single buffalo could not have maintained such a pace; it was group rhythm that sustained them. From the mass rose a low-pitched regular sound, the travel grunt, that could be heard for miles around. In the memories of all adults in the shaggy legion were pictures of the lush pastures of the north, the cool waters and breezes of the upland valleys and the peace and rest of full summer.

Twice they crossed swift rivers with never a pause. Quite automatically mothers thrust their calves on the upstream side of them so they would not be swept away on the current. Some of the smaller calves scrambled in terror upon the backs of their swimming mothers and so were ferried safely across.

As they neared their goal, the wooded country of the Yellowstone, the feeding became richer and greener. Along some of the branch valleys, old leading cows, each with a sizable following, turned aside as was the summer custom. These would not rejoin the main herd until early fall. But Kahtanka's mother was one who stayed with the herd leader.

In this long passage Kahtanka lengthened and strengthened. He had no picture of what lay ahead to lure him on but he constantly longed for the leisurely nursing and grooming that would come when each march ended. Sometimes when the pace slackened somewhat he complained loudly to his mother and was reassured by a bunt of her head.

The herds had passed the northern limits of the Bad Lands by now and were resting for a short time in the wild high country just south of the Canadian border. But all was not peace. The cowbirds were continually warning them of the approach of lobo wolves that here moved in small packs even by day and took a steady toll of cows and young. Down from the perennially white-capped mountains came occasional grizzlies following the scent strands of the herd. Slow and cumbrous as they were, they were crafty stalkers and could conceal themselves in the ambush of a meager thicket. Like brown swirling waters the herd would roll away to all sides before their sudden fearsome charges, leaving the killers standing upright eight full feet, coughing out their wrath, or more often with a dying cow or calf at their feet.

Here, like the gray wolf pack, was an arch enemy of the bison kind. Grizzlies knew all the ways of buffalo, as the buffalo knew theirs. Far back in Paleolithic times the bison had fought the prehistoric ancestors of the grizzly and the cave lion. If the killers continued to harass the herd a bull or two would move forward and give battle, and not always would the fight go to the bull. But the herd master, Kahtanka's sire, had fought many a grizzly in his time and come out victor.

One afternoon Kahtanka was frolicking stiff-legged with another calf as they took turns bunting each other off a high knob of rock in the age-old game of king-of-the-mountain. Between them and their family group a vast form suddenly uprose in the thickets. It was an old silvertip, grimmest of the grizzly kind, that had been awaiting just such a chance for an hour. Straight for the calves the grizzly lunged, still upright.

Kahtanka's playmate sounded a treble bawl of fear and her mother rushed into the breach with the heedless fury of a cow guarding her young. With scarcely an instant to spare the cow charged straight in from the side. There was a thud of bone on flesh and a roar of pain and rage. The grizzly met the attack with a full-armed blow that would have broken the back of a horse. It stopped the cow but did not down her. She bore in again, directly from the front, head low, horns at point. For a space, while the two calves scuttled to safety, the whole vast weight of the grizzly was upon the cow's back, bearing her down while the giant arms with their saber claws reached beneath her to heave and tear. Her underparts laid open, she collapsed under the weight and never rose. Even so her dying was slow and it was her agonized bellows that brought the herd master pounding down from his lookout mound.

Warned and prepared, the grizzly put all he had into a series of full-armed blows, but they had no visible effect on the king bull. The rush and upthrust of the black-horned head bowled the silvertip completely over. He was up and in again with the ponderous craft of a wrestler. Again came the sodden sound of bashing blows that lifted fur and chunks of hide but did not check for an instant the heave and thrust of the great dark head.

Each of the fighters was too grim and vast an or-

ganism to harbor such a thing as a faint-heartedness
or fear. Each harked back to an age when life was a
matter of kill or be killed and quarter was unknown.
Also each fighter was practically invulnerable and
could be conquered only by the long process of
wearing down.

As the battle grew fiercer a circle of watching buffalo gradually drew closer. Much was at stake for
them, for the loss of the leader on whom all relied
would be critical. With roarings and bellowings that
shook the ground the fighters clashed again and
again, the grizzly always agile enough to slip aside
from the full impact of the horns. He fought mostly
upreared. At times he literally rode the head and
shoulders of the herd leader, his piggish snout and
jaws and yellow saber claws working red butchery
on the bull's neck and sides.

From a protective cordon of cows Kahtanka
watched, wild-eyed and trembling in the fierce reflex
of the battle. Gradually a change came over him, a
fury that seemed to stream up out of the earth and
through him, stiffening him so that his wide black
nostrils spread and blew and his hoofs moved,
churning dirt. Then the bunt of his mother's head
brought him out of it.

At last an infinitesimal shift of chance betrayed the grizzly. In his agile shifting and dodging, the silvertip had overlooked the fact that a boulder was just behind him, and the herd bull's horns suddenly spitted the enemy, pinning him to the rock. Rip and heave and writhe as the grizzly would, the horns worked deeper and deeper into his vitals with cunning twist and pull until the savage life spark finally went out. A concerted bellow swept the watching herd, very different from the bawling that accompanied the blood smell of their own kind. An ancient enemy and one of the fiercest had been vanquished.

After all was over there was the bawling complaint of the little female whose mother had been killed. Her piteous outcry went on and on as she raced desperately from cow to cow. The head of every mother bent to her consolingly and rough black tongues came out to dab at her. By nightfall she was the adopted offspring of four or five cows, chief among them Kahtanka's own mother. She was amply fed and numerous tongues licked and curried and groomed her until her grieving was silenced in the bliss of constant attention.

Next day she had her milk whenever and where-ever she pleased, taking turns with other calves and even getting preference over them. Only once or twice did she voice her grieving note like a dying echo. Most often she came and shared Kahtanka's meal. At first he resented it, bunting her off, but his mother welcomed the orphan and as the days passed Kahtanka accepted her too, and they played continually together. Even so the other mothers and some young cows without calves continued their comforting of the lonely one, caressing and combing her so that her coat had many times more grooming than any other calf's.

By late summer the constant lickings, cardings and curryings of her many foster mothers had turned the orphan's coat to down and silk in comparison to other calves which had to get along with a single mother. Her very curls had been licked straight so that her red-brown coat was like the fur of a beaver. Even the wool of her shoulders was clean-combed and had a fluff and gloss that was to remain through the years and give her her name, Beaverskin.

SEPTEMBER found the herd fat with summer feeding, coats coming into prime, calves full of frolic and the young bulls combative for the rutting season now at hand. Kahtanka and other bull calves followed the example of their elders, straining head to head, butting and snorting and often leaping stiff-legged into the air with exuberance. None of the calves knew what they were fighting for, but they pushed and strained, drew off and cracked together again with a sound like breaking sticks.

The cows that had summered apart were drifting in and terrific battles began taking place between the weathered bulls. Some of the old timers battled the sun out of one sky and the moon out of another with still no definite advantage on either side. In the midst of all this furor a pack train brought white hunters into the region and the sportsmen carried on a mounted hunt along the flat sandy reaches of the river.

The spring calves knew their first mad terror at the roar of the magazine rifle and the demon's scream of unseen bullets in the air. As part of the herd swept away in flight, a few calves were separated from their mothers. Finding themselves alone they hid their heads in bushes or whatever they could find, if only a tussock of grass, believing they were hid from sight, though their trembling hind quarters arched ludicrously in full view.

One of Kahtanka's butting companions was wounded in this hunt and lay in the thickets bawling piteously. In the face of unknown terrors his family turned back for him. A bullet had pierced his hind leg but his mother and another cow heaved him upright and, supporting his hind quarters between them, piloted him back to the woods where he could be fed and cared for.

By October all was quiet and orderly once more and the herd turned south along its well-worn trails. A fearsome time awaited them, for all along the southern passage Indians and settlers would be waiting to take their big fall toll of meat and hides for the coming winter. Still farther south there would be the wagon trains of the pioneers and out from each line of wagons a few hunters would ride to make their kills. The bison sensed the death and peril in store, yet were braced and keyed like soldiers to meet what must come.

CHAPTER FOUR
Crow Boy

THE OGLALA SIOUX were riding north early this fall to meet the buffalo coming south, for Standing Elk and some of the elders saw signs of a severe winter ahead. Much pemmican and many hides would be needed.

The night before, a small band of Minniconjou hunters had stopped at the camp. Old friends of the Oglala, they had been asked to join in the hunt. Now in the gray of dawn the women were furling the white skin tents, lashing the tent poles to the saddles of the pack horses and tying the rest of the camp baggage on the *travois*, long, hidebound poles which dragged behind the pack horses. Hawk and the other boys had already rounded up the stock. Now they stood about watching the preparations of the hunters or wrestling and vying in feats of strength with the young Minniconjou. As the lodges came down, the thin, wolfish Oglala dogs moved here and there searching for scraps. They would follow the march as always and at times be used to carry packs.

When the hunting party set out, the visiting Minniconjou rode at the head, according to polite custom. After these came the chiefs and some of the elders of the Oglala. The women and children and pack animals brought up the rear, while on either side rode a protective cordon of young warriors arrayed in feathers and paint and carrying their bows and arrows and plumed lances. As they rode, they sang war-like songs of bravery made up by the Strong Hearts, that small society of picked warriors of whom Sitting Bull of the Hunkpapa was head man. Hawk watched the warriors enviously, listening to their songs, singing them under his breath, memorizing them.

With him Hawk carried his man-size bow and arrows for, since the killing of the young buffalo, he had his hunter's reputation to maintain. All that summer he had practiced until he could place three arrows in the space of a small knot and his bow arm was almost as strong as a grown man's. His father had given him for his own the fast piebald pony on which he had made his spring kill. Cetan, he had named him, meaning The Swift. Mounted on Cetan, Hawk would leave the line of march at intervals and ride out seeking game for the communal pot.

On the third afternoon of this march Hawk sighted a buck and doe crossing a far hill. Here was meat worthy of any hunter. The ten-tined buck had doubtless been hunted much, and would take long stalking. Hawk pressed his horse around the left flank of the hill, hoping to surprise the deer, but they were wary and had sped half a mile down a ravine on the opposite slope. The instant he appeared they saw him.

Hawk sat stone still until the deer fell to feeding again, then he pressed Cetan warily downgrade through sparse timber, stopping and starting again like a feeding deer. The way led through light and shadow over the brown and gold of fallen leaves. Cetan understood. Sure-footed, he avoided every stone and fallen branch, pausing at just the right times, without even a signal from the boy.

Now Hawk was moving around and away from

the game, but the still hunt must bring him in time within the general path of the drifting deer. When he had emerged at last at the top of a brushy ravine he had cut down the distance by half. The deer were still feeding, but the buck's antlered head was lifting from moment to moment, sensing something. Again without any signal Cetan froze. Moments later, at a whispered word and a pressure on the thong bridle, he backed downward in his own tracks. Presently Hawk left him in a clump of willows and began his final stalk on foot. The breeze was with him and that was all he needed, for he had long since learned to move through thickets or even dry leaves with a wildcat's stealth.

He was lying still as a snake beneath a low spruce when the deer in their feeding emerged upon the bare crest of the ridge. Hawk waited endlessly, arrow set to bow, until the buck's shoulder turned his way. The bowstring sang and, as the arrow struck, the buck leapt high, then plunged away down the far slope. The doe simply disappeared like a wisp of smoke.

Hawk ran back to Cetan. Soon they were following the blood marks on ground and leaves. The buck was far ahead, still covering ground between the measured squeezes of the heart. Already Hawk had wandered too far from the line of march, he knew, and the sun was sinking fast. But it never occurred to him to turn back.

Now the blood trail was clearer, the spots larger and closer together. Hawk's arrow was a good one, keen enough to work in and in as the quarry ran. The pace of the animal had slowed; the laboring heart was working its own end.

It was in the orange light of the setting sun that Hawk almost overran the dying buck, so well was it hidden, blent with the earth and shadow between two rocks. He loosed another arrow from the saddle, but first he spoke to the Deer Spirit, according to the custom of his people.

IT WAS owl-light and Hawk was skinning out the kill when an echo not of the forest struck upon some nerve of hearing. Too slight actually to register as sound, nonetheless it had roused him utterly. Somewhere over the ridge above him were men not of his people. The only visible effect on Hawk was a swifter, surer stroke of his knife. He cut out a hind quarter for packing in before he crept to the rim of rock above to peer.

On the plain below he saw a large Indian hunting party making camp for the night, the squaws already pitching the tipis. By their blankets and head-dress Hawk knew them to be Crows, ancient enemies of the Sioux. They, too, must be seeking the main buffalo trails ahead of the usual season, but this was Sioux territory and such poaching called for battle. Taking only the dressed-out haunch of the venison with him, he got to his horse and headed Cetan back toward the line of march.

Hawk now carried news as well as meat, news that might rate a *coup,* but he had strayed far afield and night was already upon him. He knew his direction as well as any wild thing, but in the blackness he had to let Cetan pick the trail. At last, from a rise of ground, he saw the gleam of the Oglala camp fires. Singing and the muffled throb of a drum came to him as he drew closer. His people had no suspicion of enemies so near. It disturbed him to realize that the whole camp might have been surprised and killed by the Crows if he had not tracked his deer to its dying.

Wood Mouse and his mother saw him as he came into camp and cried out because he had been gone so long. But Hawk rode straight past to the lodge of the war chief. Horned Thunder's eyes went over the bloodied arms of the young hunter and then to his tense face as Hawk told what he had seen without the waste of a word. Raven, a herald sitting by the lodge fire, was sent out at once with the news. In a few minutes Hawk was the center of a dozen or more of the head men and an eager group of young warriors. The warriors, who had been singing war songs for weeks, were all for attacking the Crow camp at once, but Horned Thunder restrained them. A council was called in the chief's lodge and Standing Elk was asked to make medicine. After smoking and singing, the *shaman* opened his medicine bag and tossed the painted sticks in air. The red one for war fell pointing east, to the dawn. He counseled a surprise attack at the pre-dawn hour when even the watch of wild things grows lax. To this Horned Thunder agreed.

That night Hawk was given his first *coup* stick for the warning he had brought. This meant that he might win honors among fighting men for killing an enemy or for being the first or even the second to touch a fallen enemy, or for stealing an enemy horse. A boy who won the right to count *coup* early in life accumulated honors and so had a better chance of becoming a famed warrior or even a chief. But there was no feast for him, for this was a night of no fires in the Oglala camp, a night of silence and preparation.

IN TWO PARTIES under Horned Thunder and White Antelope, the Sioux rode forth in the darkness of earliest morning. The eleven visiting Minniconjou warriors were with them. Hawk was allowed to accompany the two scouts who went ahead, because he knew the exact position of the enemy. Before the first dove tints of the false dawn, all the Sioux were drawn up behind the line of hills just above the Crow camp. Only one tethered dog gave warning as the Sioux swept down-grade at a pelting gallop, their war-whoops cutting the air like wolf cries, the ground reverberating under the pounding hoofs of their mounts.

The Sioux had the advantage of complete surprise. The Crows burst from their tipis in wild confusion, their fighting men unable to form a single compact phalanx. They split into groups, the warriors on foot pressed back to back, a few already mounted on their war horses, others standing behind horses that had been picketed close by their tipis.

Everywhere horses were rearing and whinnying and dogs skulking and being stumbled over. Wailing and crying, the women began fleeing off across the plain, pulling their frightened children after them. Some of the old men had mounted and were covering the squaws' retreat to the hills where they could hide. When the fighting was over the remaining warriors would join them there, for after much killing no camp was ever returned to.

Even in the near dark the Sioux's first screaming charge brought down many of the hastily rallied enemy. The braves swept past on either side, circled, and then came in again. They rode in close formation, shouting out the Strong Heart songs of their warrior society. It was a field day for them, a chance to retaliate for many a Crow raid of the past and to break the spirit of an ancient enemy. A third charge broke and swerved aside, leaving more dead behind, some of them their own. The Crow fighters were already standing knee-deep among their fallen. A few had tried desperately to escape on horseback, but were brought down by Sioux riders who circled the whole field of battle.

Wild with excitement, Hawk galloped Cetan behind or on the flanks of charge after charge of the

fighting men. He would have been in their midst
with his new *coup* stick had not Horned Thunder
twice warned him off. But no one could keep him
from following after, and he was learning much, seeing Sioux warfare at its bloodiest and grimmest and
finding that he did not quail. He had no shield, no
war club, only his unused bow and arrow and *coup*
stick, but the speed and power of Cetan worked with
him and three times he counted second *coup* on a
dying enemy's shoulder, each time witnessed by
nearby Sioux warriors.

The Crows were beginning to sing their death
songs now, for they were outnumbered and could
see the hopeless turn of the battle. One Crow warrior, a sub-chief with two eagle feathers upright in
his hair, had charged out again and again on his war
horse with such fury that no Sioux had elected to
close with him in a death clash. Finally, his horse
wounded, the Crow chief stood facing his attackers
on the outer edge of the diminishing knot of Crow
fighters.

Hawk had been watching this brave man with admiration, for such courage was thrilling even in an
enemy. Now the Crow chief's horse had dropped
under him and he was making his last stand. Hawk

saw a tall slim boy about his own age run forward to stand at the warrior's side. They were father and son, Hawk guessed, for their two proud, unflinching faces were much alike. They were ready to meet death together. The warrior chief was singing in a strong challenging voice and the boy with him. Neither so much as changed expression as the Sioux swept forward a final time.

Men had fallen on either side of the two when the death song of the brave Crow chief suddenly ceased. His eyes still fiercely open, he leaned slightly forward and fell like a tree and Hawk could see that he had been standing in a pool of his own blood. He had literally died on his feet. The boy still stood straight and proud, neither crying nor asking for mercy. Hawk knew suddenly that he could not bear to have him die. He sliced his pony through a closing ring of fighters, slipped to the ground and flung himself in front of the Crow boy, arms spread wide in protection.

"Let this one live!" he cried out. "This one is too brave to die!"

Arrows and lances were momentarily stayed, but the blood of the Sioux warriors was up. They were killing right and left, no quarter for any. They circled and came in from the other side. Hawk moved swiftly round to face them from the opposite direction, his arms still spread.

"This one is my brother!" he called out loudly. "I take him! I have no other brother!"

White Antelope, who had stopped his war horse close before Hawk, gave a grunt of approval, but Hurries-To-War and Pretty Weasel, another young hot-head, circled again and would have killed the boy had not Hawk kept putting his body between. At moments when he had to move quickly, Hawk faced the Crow boy and what he saw in the valiant black eyes was like an answer or a counterpart to his own fiery spirit. Once, as he turned, their hands touched briefly and it seemed to seal a pact between them.

Still the matter hung in the balance because of the kill-crazed young men and Hawk continued to stand close guard. When the fighting ceased, White Antelope spoke in Hawk's behalf, but it was not until Horned Thunder came up that the order was given which ensured the Crow boy's life.

CHAPTER FIVE

Time of Great Change

SIX HUNDRED miles had the herd covered in its recent wanderings, from the Powder and the Yellowstone in Montana to the Rio Grande and the Arizona-New Mexico border, following the well-worn buffalo trails. Now it was November again, but still clear and bright and very dry in the piñon-clad hills above the Rio Grande. The river was low at this time and the herd had easily forded the stream at a familiar crossing. A full day and night that process had taken. Now the great mass stretched for twenty miles on every side, peppering the tawny hills like the piñons themselves. For days the buffalo had lingered here, not wanting to leave the abundance of water and feeding for the final dry leg of their passage.

In the early morning light a long, slow line of wagons appeared on the mesa to the east. Though the wagons were still several miles away, a mere thread on the dun plain, the old herd master was already aware of their approach. He could not see them but the wind was from that direction and from time to time it brought to his broad black nostrils the scent of man—and something more. As he ruminated, munching the sun-browned bunch grass, he would stop and swing his head again and again toward the slow-crawling caravan, still invisible to him but ever more disturbing.

Ever since the battle with the grizzly the herd master had been lame in one foreleg and slightly slowed, but his awareness had become sharpened to balance this. At mid-morning the leader moved down to the river and drank, then stood awhile in the shallows. When he returned to his look-out hill the alarming smell was much more distinct. No mistaking it now; it was the smell of death. There was a stirring in the ranks as others caught it.

In the midst of his family clan Kahtanka was reacting violently, young as he was. Sounding his treble bawl of fear and alarm, he began pawing the earth and bunting his mother, his many aunts, and his adopted sister, as if no less than a pair of grizzlies was attacking the band. He was almost two now and tall as a pony, a good size larger than any other calf born the same spring and showing unmistakably the line of the master bull. He kept sounding his tocsin of alarm until an older bull came and disciplined him. Later the breeze shifted again and the smell was forgotten, fear drowning in the immemorial sense of numbers.

As the wagons came nearer, the section of the herd that had been grazing on the river bank rolled quietly back into the hills. At this point the herd master also gave a warning signal and the ranks around him withdrew like an ebbing tide to more distant heights where the dark piñons thickened protectively.

Down below, the tarpaulin-covered wagons forded the stream where the bison had crossed. Horses were unspanned and presently saddled. Men began riding slowly up the slopes, spreading out quietly below the flanks of the herd. Each man carried two guns. They did not ride in among the buffalo as the Indians and settlers often did; instead these men left their horses at some distance and moved into the thickets on foot, each choosing a stand within gunshot. Then the rifles began to speak, such rifles as no Indian or wagon-train settler ever possessed, roaring out not once but again and again in rapid succession.

Each man had chosen his position with craft and each shot as fast as he could pull trigger six times and reload. The nearer section of the herd went swirling and sweeping back toward the hills, but these rifles carried death for over a thousand yards. Two minor stampedes began but were stopped by the skill of the riflemen, who brought down the animals in the van of each. The fallen ones blocked the rush, terrifying those coming after and turning the tide back upon itself. Again and again this process was repeated, the foremost bison brought down by the hunters nearest in line, until, in complete pandemonium, a great section of the herd was churning round and round in directionless panic.

Thereafter all the riflemen fired into the mass as fast as fresh ammunition could be loaded. When one rifle grew too hot to handle it was dropped and the second gun went into play. Some of the hunters poured water from canteens through the barrels of their guns to cool them.

More than four hundred bison were killed within a short space that afternoon before a concerted flight took the frothing, white-eyed mass over the hills and out of range. The riflemen then returned to their camp by the river, leaving a detachment of skinners at work on the carcasses.

Next morning without particular haste the rifle-men rode after the herd, the skinners following with the hide wagons. Behind them the skinned carcasses lay strewn along the slopes. No more than a haunch or two of meat and a few tongues and hearts had been taken from all the slain buffalo, for these men were not sportsmen in any sense but commercial hunters who killed only for the money the hides would bring in eastern markets.

All that morning the mounted hide hunters har-ried the herd, bringing down scores of animals each time they came within range, then following on as if the hunt were only beginning. As was to be ex-pected, a good stand was increasingly harder to come by today, for the herd was somewhat warier. But working methodically and in unison the hunters achieved one stand after another as the day wore on.

Along the back trail overworked skinners vied with flocks of carrion birds and were only a little ahead of the coyotes and wolves.

AFTER THE first bloody stand was over, the master bull drove his following a good four miles into the hills. Sounds of firing finally ceased from behind; the hunt was over, and darkness was falling. All through the ranks there was a trembling of shock and reaction, for there had never been so much killing among them, and the cries of the disabled and dying were still in their ears, the blood-death smell still on the breeze. Other wings of the herd which had been under direct attack were drawing in, among them many wounded voicing their pain in low mutters and bellowings. Also there were calls and crying from those who had lost their nearest ones.

But now darkness and their own numbers consoled them. And this night there were no attacks of night prowlers at the edges of the herd, for the killer packs all gorged upon the newly skinned carcasses on the slopes below.

In the intense cold of the small hours the herd bunched for warmth, even the cowbirds settling

closer into the wool of their hosts. The only mist of
the clear autumn morning that followed was that of
the herds' own warmth rising in the first light. Within this the cowbirds lifted in air and settled again
with rasping cries. The young calves, always the first
astir, cavorted out into the open where frost had
crusted the bunch grass with a silvery shine, but
dashed quickly back again to the body warmth of
their family clans and the comfort of breakfast.

Kahtanka, who had bedded apart with some
young bulls, sought out his mother in the first light.
She lay in a depression with Beaverskin beside her,
no welcome or invitation to him as he came up. It
was becoming clearer and clearer to Kahtanka that
he was not wanted here, but this morning he had a
particularly urgent thirst. He lowered his chunky
head and gave his mother a bunt by way of re-
minder, but she did not stir. Stubborn and angry, he
redoubled his efforts. Abruptly his mother was on
her feet and he found himself ignominiously tossed
by a sweep of her black-horned head. The white
gleam of her rolling eye warned him further that
there would be no compromise now or any other
time; he was weaned. This final rebuff was made the
more rankling by the sight of Beaverskin eyeing him

placidly without even moving from her bedding place.

Wrathful, Kahtanka returned to the clique of young bulls in whose company he had been thrown of late and clashed skulls with another two-year-old, a familiar butting companion. In a minute or two he had overthrown that one, pawed the ground victoriously, and tackled another spike bull who stood watching. It was only after several such tussles that Kahtanka was ravenous enough to essay a breakfast of frosted bunch grass.

Before the sun had yet warmed the slopes there came sounds that stopped all feeding: far slapping reports of rifles began again and went on and on as they had the day before. Instantly the herd master sprang to life, rallying his following with urgent bellows, heaving and bunting the flanks of the nearest. Kahtanka, too, was fired as before and helped to drive the laggards. But not even the herd master could imagine that these hunters would follow on and on—not even now that it was happening could he believe it, because in the past hunters had never done this. As the present hunt continued with the mounted riflemen on their flanks, the various herd leaders carried out the short, erratic flights that had

sufficed through the centuries, always coming to rest
again in the belief that it was now ended. On this,
of course, the hide hunters counted and methodically carried on their lethal work whenever the fleeing
mass came to rest. They counted also on the panic
that would eventually result from their repeated
attacks, a vast and almost suicidal confusion that
must play directly into their hands.

Even greater than they could have foreseen was
the tragic debacle that occurred at midday. A low
thunder began to fill the air. It mounted and grew
till the earth vibrated and a veil of powdery dust
rose over the close-pressed herd. Maddened by pursuit and death on every side, the bison had launched
en masse into headlong stampede. At first it was only
the wing of the herd nearest the riflemen, then thousands of animals were swept into the heedless surge,
the thundering panic of it rising until it possessed
all. Quickly it became a flight which could not slow.
The pressure of the multitude accumulated and behind all rode the hunters, yelling and occasionally
shooting into the mass.

Piñons and scrub junipers were snapped off and
ground to splinters beneath the churning hoofs.
Only for great boulders did the ranks split and

sweep around. Many animals went down in the
close-pressed flow and were overridden. When the
high rocky cliff overlooking the Rio Grande was
reached, the front ranks saw the peril too late. They
tried to swerve and break their rush but the momen-
tum of the thousands behind swept them on and
over the sheer seventy-foot drop to their deaths. In
spite of the warning bellows from ahead nearly three
thousand animals pitched to the rocks below before
a thinning of the ranks permitted a parting and
turning of the herd to either side. Hundreds of animals were not killed outright in the fall. Cushioned
by the many bodies beneath, they sprawled with
broken legs, necks or backs, bellowing in pain and
doomed to a slow death unless the hunters came and
hastened the end.

From another far cliff overlooking the river the
band under Kahtanka's sire listened to the sounds
and smelled the smells of dying and agony of their
kind, and later heard in the clear air echoes of shouts
and orders when the hide wagons drew up to the
scene of carnage. Only that fierce urgency for flight
which had burned in the herd master had saved
them, leading him down a canyon remembered of
old, well before the stampede started. All his band

and many others that had fallen in behind them escaped the actual slaughter, but all were suffering. A
concerted bawling rose now from their numbers,
more a sounding of grief and loss than of fear. They
waited on, as if expecting their dead to rejoin them.
All through the afternoon of that terrible day and
the night that followed they waited.

In the herd master, standing moveless and apart
on his high crest, a slow and terrible wrath was rising
against this new kind of hunting that had no end and
drove all mad. It was buffalo spirit to clash with any
obstacle, even welcoming opposition and never giving up, but this new enemy was outside the law of
nature and could not be fought in any known way.

Kahtanka felt the new terror in the air and joined
the others in the voicing of grief and loss. But mostly
it was his own private woe that rankled him. Yesterday's repulse by his mother had been final, and the
shock of it had blended quickly with the fearsome
tumult of the day. Willy-nilly a bull among bulls
now, he focalized upon the herd master himself. His
sire was the biggest and the bravest, and all the
other bulls kept looking at him, awaiting his slightest
signal. Now, as he stood brooding, head low, his long
black beard touched the ground and the coarse hair

on his forelegs swayed in the breeze. He was six feet
high at his matted hump and fully ten feet long.
Drawing near, Kahtanka was suddenly overawed.
He simply stood there, staring.

N E X T M O R N I N G the scattered remnants of the
herd flowed together again and resumed their southward passage. Always hereafter they would avoid
this well-known river ford, for the dark Miocene
cliffs above had become a place of evil memory.

All that day the death smell followed them on
the northwest wind and dark-winged birds sailed
overhead in the opposite direction, or funneled
slowly into sight from high sky. Never before had
they come in such numbers. All pursuit had stopped.
The hide hunters had remained with the heaped
carcasses at the foot of the cliff, racing with corrup-
tion, flies, and scavengers to garner their treasure of
robes.

The march of the herd was due south now, keeping to the deep-worn trails that the bison kind had
made, which followed the most natural and easiest
ways in a rugged land. For a time now they re-
achieved their old rhythm of movement, much faster

than the spring journey, for there were no young calves to slow them, and the travel grunt rose steadily in the air. In most of the herd recent tribulations were soon erased, for in the blood of all was the knowledge that the females of the band already carried the seed for another spring's calving.

CHAPTER SIX

The Bald-Face

BECAUSE OF the unprecedented killing on the
southwestern plains the buffalo had come north early
this year, and the Oglala had followed them to the
Yellowstone. It was now April and snow still lay on
the northern slopes along the river. The tribe had
come up from the Black Hills country as always,
taking their meat as they came, antelope on the
plains, and deer and elk along the Porcupine and
Yellowstone. Neither meat nor skins were prime this
time of year, but they must eat. Up here in the buffalo's summering ground it was like the far-past days
that the old men told about, when there were always
buffalo about and never any hurry about laying in

skins or pemmican. The hunters brought in only enough meat for the day itself from the widely scattered herd.

It was here that spring that Standing Elk happened to see Kahtanka again. He was a chunky, half-grown bull now, so that it was only the white star mark on the forehead that identified him. This, combined with his dark color and the *shaman's* own sure feeling was enough. Good medicine would come from this encounter and thankfulness filled the *shaman's* heart. He renewed his prayers to *Wahkan-Tanka* for the protection of the black one.

That spring Hawk and Crow Boy made many separate hunts of their own. Following the battle of his people with the Sioux, Crow Boy had been formally adopted by Standing Elk as a son, and by Hawk as a brother, a simple ceremony witnessed by the chief and elders of the tribe. Crow Boy was a Sioux now in all but his name, and that, as everyone knew, he would soon win for himself, for his courage was unquestionable.

A year of growing up together in the lodge of Standing Elk had brought Hawk and Crow Boy closer together than if they had been blood brothers. Real brothers are apt to take each other for granted, but with these two there was not only deep mutual admiration but a continual striving to live up to it, a kind of vying to grow in each other's eyes. Each boy had already counted war *coups* and made a hunting record for himself.

The fall before, on the Bighorn River, they had met a white trapper who had an old rifle to trade. For thirty prime beaver skins carefully stretched and scraped he would consider parting with an old Sharps muzzle-loading rifle. Crow Boy said from the first that the white trapper had a forked tongue, but Hawk greatly desired a gun and if they missed this chance to acquire one it might be years before such an opportunity came again. Getting the thirty skins was a big undertaking, for they had their daily tasks about camp to attend to, but snaring by night and by day for miles up and down river they met the trapper's price, plus a sack of powder and a lesson apiece in the priming and loading of the gun, which had seen its best days long before.

On this April day the boys had been out hunting since early morning but had sighted nothing worthy of a shot from their prize possession. Only a very special quarry would rate the expenditure of a charge of powder from their very limited supply. A bull elk or a caribou, perhaps, Hawk said, or a demon wolverine, strong medicine for any hunter.

Both were mounted. Hawk carried the gun low and balanced in his right hand. He loved the weight of it and its very cumbersomeness, for it was longer and heavier than any of the nine guns his tribe possessed. Crow Boy had his bow and arrow and a long-bladed butcher knife, originally from Fort Laramie, ground down to a thin sharp curve by much honing.

"I saw his teeth also," Crow Boy said, out of a long silence.

Hawk did not need to ask whose teeth. Early that morning Crow Boy had told him his dream about the white trapper: how the bearded, grizzled face had hung before him with a mocking grin.

"In my dream you and I were straining and panting," Crow Boy said. "We will have to fight something today."

Hawk's gaze met his foster brother's understandingly. He had learned long since to respect the other's dream-telling.

"I hope it will be something new," he said.

"It will be," replied Crow Boy. "New and bad, like that white man."

Hawk took cheer, for it had begun to seem as if their hunt today might net them nothing.

Presently they came in sight of buffalo, a straggling band stretched out over three low hills. They tethered their horses and moved along the outermost fringe of the herd, but they were not hunting buffalo today. The animals seemed to know it, for they were almost as oblivious as cattle, except when some guardian bull would raise his head sharply to gaze at them before resuming his feeding.

It was Crow Boy who sighted a young she-buffalo with a silky, gold-brown coat that gleamed in the sunlight like one of the prime beavers they had taken on the Bighorn.

"Look," he said. "A beaver robe, such as the old men tell of. Never have I seen one before."

"Truly, it would be something to make talk around the night fires," Hawk said, hesitating; for perhaps it would be well to take this one.

"If we were hunting buffalo," Crow Boy pointed out. "But there is plenty of meat in camp."

They walked on quietly through the trees until a dark patch of shadow moved abruptly on the slope to the left, showing as a huge grizzly sitting up in the undergrowth. As the bear turned to face them the grayish patch of fur that ran like a blaze-mark across its brow showed it to be an old bald-face from the high mountains, the most ferocious of the grizzly kind. This was the one beast on which the Sioux counted *coup* as on a human enemy.

Quite evidently the grizzly had been stalking the buffalo herd. Early spring was not usually a time for grizzlies. This one must have just undenned from his winter hibernation, or else was one of those savage old males who out of sheer ill temper elect to wander abroad all year, subsisting on whatever lean fare the winter woods afforded.

"Hau!" breathed Hawk softly. His hand reached out to Crow Boy. Neither took his eyes off the bear, for there was never any knowing what a grizzly would do.

After a moveless interval the bear, instead of melting into the thickets, dropped to all fours and advanced, ears flattened, its little eyes glaring like gray steel. It meant to attack and both boys knew that flight would be fatal to one of them. They could not reach their horses. Even though they ran their fastest the grizzly could overtake them in the brush; if they took to the trees one of them would be scooped off before he had climbed ten feet. But in fact there was not the remotest idea of running in either of them.

Hawk clutched the rifle tighter and Crow Boy drew his knife, for at this distance the best-driven arrow would merely have precipitated a charge. Without words and close together the two moved sidewise and backward into a cleared space between trees, the instinctive maneuver of fighters picking the best spot to do battle.

As they backed away Hawk saw to the rifle's cap and priming pan, then took aim with the bear less than sixty feet away and coming on. As they had learned, the old Sharps would fire five or six times and fail the seventh time, but you couldn't even count on that—it might be the fourth or the eighth time. This was one of the bad times, for nothing happened at the trigger pull.

"I will keep him busy while you look to the gun," Crow Boy said softly. He stepped in front of Hawk, pressing him back with one hand. While Hawk moved off on a diagonal course, working desperately with new cap and ramrod, Crow Boy stood facing the grizzly, uttering some brave grunts.

Abruptly now the bear dropped to all fours. They could no longer see it but they knew by the move-

ment of the bushes that the grizzly, though circuit-
ous about it, was coming even closer. Crow Boy held
his ground, facing the rustling, waving bushes. His
eye was on the exact spot when the bald-face rose
up on its hind quarters again, no more than ten yards
in front of him.

For a space the bear held its pose, reared a good
five feet above the brush, the front paws with their
yellow saber claws dangling on the matted chest. As
Crow Boy stood there waiting, there came an inter-
ruption—a terrified whinnying from one of the tethered ponies. The grizzly's head swung in the direction of the sound, short ears pricked with savage
alertness. Then there was the thud of hoofbeats and
panicky snorting, diminishing in the distance. The
horses had scented the grizzly and bolted.

From the tail of his eye Crow Boy saw that Hawk
now had the rifle ready. Then the crashing report of
the Sharps filled the woods and a puff of white
smoke swirled above Hawk, who had been almost
knocked off his feet by the recoil. The grizzly clawed
at its own chest and sounded its terrible fighting
roar: "Hough! Hough! Hough!"

The bald-face came fast then, breasting through
the thickets with strange overhand swimming strokes

of the forepaws above the brush. Once in the open it hurled itself toward Hawk, the heavy hide rolling and swaying on back and shoulders.

Crow Boy saw Hawk holding his ground with clubbed gun, voicing a strong war shout. Joining in the shout, Crow Boy leapt in with drawn knife. Swift as its charge was there had to be the moment when the grizzly paused and squatted back to deliver the smashing forearm blow which was its most lethal stroke. Crow Boy counted upon this, also upon the extra length of Hawk's rifle to bludgeon with. Of nothing else did he think except the blade of his knife and the position of the bear's heart.

Before the grizzly could squat back, the butt of Hawk's rifle thudded upon its snout and Crow Boy was in from the left, sinking his knife with all his strength into the bear's side, turning the blade, wrenching it out, and leaping back almost in the same breath. With a roar like close thunder the grizzly struck a boxer's blow that would have felled a horse, but the second that it took to squat for the stroke gave Hawk a margin of inches for another blow with his gun. Then, as one, the boys backed and dodged toward a great jumble of boulders, for once among the rocks Hawk might have a chance to reload the rifle.

But as he lifted the heavy weapon to swing again his foot turned on a stone and he was down on his back, kicking desperately at the red froth-flaked jaws of the grizzly hanging above him. In the final instant Crow Boy's lean, coppery body flashed between, his knife sinking again to the hilt, this time close to the heart.

The pain of the stab turned the grizzly bellowing upon the wielder of the knife. The bear flung forward in a waddling rush and one mailed paw caught Crow Boy a glancing blow that spun him four yards away like a blown leaf. The bald-face was right on him and now it was Crow Boy kicking upward at the vast, overhanging snout. The grizzly merely opened its mouth, closed its jaws upon a flying foot, and held.

Gun thrown aside, Hawk came in with drawn knife. As he did so Crow Boy was snatched up. Head down, he hung dangling by one leg from the grizzly's jaws, but with his knife still clutched in his right hand. Writhing and doubling upward, he stabbed fiercely again and again into the beast's belly. At every stab the bear let out a stifled roar, but did not release the imprisoned foot.

Now with its vast forepaws the bald-face drew Crow Boy's body up against its chest, for a death hug. Leaping and reaching, Hawk sank his knife twice into the bear's neck, both times twisting the blade. Strangling on the gush of blood in its throat, the grizzly dropped Crow Boy and in the madness of its death agony began tearing chunks of fur from its several wounds. In its struggles it charged blindly into a nearby tree.

Hawk got Crow Boy, dripping with bear's blood, to his feet and half lifted, half dragged him back among the boulders. Then he retrieved his rifle and squatted to reload it. Crow Boy was down on one knee trying to stop the bleeding of his torn foot and ankle. Below them was a great threshing among the bushes, a succession of hoarse, choking coughs, each feebler than the last, and finally silence.

Hawk and Crow Boy smiled into each other's strained, blood-smeared faces.

"We have overcome that one!" Hawk said.

"Now we count *coup*. You first," said Crow Boy.

"No, you," Hawk said.

Leaning on Hawk's shoulder, Crow Boy limped

and hopped down to the kill, but refused to count first *coup* on the eight-foot monster. Sprawled there gape-jawed, with outflung paws, the bald-face looked vaster now than in life. The two stood side by side, Crow Boy on one foot, looking down at this worsted foe, the most terrible that the mountain wilderness contained. Both had been bathed in its blood and according to Sioux belief were now infused with the courage and strength of the fallen one. It was a solemn moment. Then Hawk turned to his injured friend.

"Now I will find your horse and bring him back."

"But we will not leave until we have skinned this one out," Crow Boy said stoutly.

THEY FINISHED skinning out their prize by the light of the spring moon that rose late over the high forest. Very carefully they cut out the grizzly's yellow claws to be made into a bear-claw necklace, the most cherished of treasures. In spite of the poultice of fungus and leaves which Hawk had made for him by the stream bank, Crow Boy was in great pain from his torn and shattered ankle. Although Hawk had found their horses, they were far from camp and by common consent they lay down to sleep in the tent-like shelter of a hemlock.

They did not arrive at camp next day until the hour when the horses went down to water. The sight of the boys' scarred torsos, Crow Boy's chewed and swollen ankle, and the huge pelt of the grizzly lying across the back of Hawk's pony with head and paws attached, sent Two Tomahawk, one of the heralds, running ahead of them through camp with loud cries. It was for such outcry, bringing word of brave deeds or of danger, that the Sioux heart was ever waiting. At the first sound of it work ceased, the lodges emptied, warriors gathered in the aisles between the tipis, and women and girls clapped hands over their mouths in awe and amazement.

By this time two chanting warriors were leading the ponies of Hawk and Crow Boy and children were running behind. This was such a story as told itself; no witness was even needed. To behold these victors was to begin a mighty celebration. Name-making history had been made that day and would now be sung. Not only were Hawk and Crow Boy eligible for new names and an eagle feather for each for bravery, but this day itself would be named for their deed in the Sioux calendar: The-Day-That-Brothers-Fought-The-Bear.

According to custom Standing Elk called out loudly for all to hear that his two sons had brought honor to his lodge and to the tribe, but it was Chief Horned Thunder himself who called for the black paint of high achievement. Two of the tribe's best fighting men decorated the victors, while the squaws prepared the feast, which would go on all that day and night. All this before Standing Elk could get Crow Boy into the Medicine Lodge for the treatment of his wounds with mosses, herbs and prayers. Later, by the fires, as the heroes were handed choice tidbits of buffalo hump and tongue or browned pemmican larded with tallow, rich in their ears sounded the ululating cries of the girls and young women, the hero-calls coveted by every young warrior.

Next day, in Standing Elk's lodge, both boys were given new honorary names to be accepted if they chose. For a second time Hawk kept his own first name which had been given to him by his father, but Crow Boy was glad to accept the new Sioux name which identified him with his adopted people: Stabs-The-Bear.

Even before the ceremony was over, the newly

named Stabs-The-Bear had become very ill. His injured leg was badly swollen and infected and his eyes were overbright with fever. Standing Elk chanted long over him and made medicine the rest of that day. Another day and the boy's heat was only greater and he was saying strange things, calling them all by names they did not know. The powers of Standing Elk were strained, quivering to their limit against the poison enemy in the boy's blood. That afternoon he left Willow Woman to watch the sick one and went into the hills in search of certain herbs he knew, also to pray alone.

For days Hawk hung close, sorrowing and missing his friend, then a buffalo hunt with the young men drew him away. That day he was invited by Hurries-To-War and some of the other fighting men to join the Oglala warrior society, the Strong Hearts. He came back from that first meeting with his hair tied up on his forehead in a warrior's coiffure. He was young for such an honor. To belong to this society meant close association with men older than himself. Theirs was a code of utter fearlessness, of death rather than retreat. Each member consented as a trial to be tied fast to a tree or rock during a battle or under fire. The only way to gain prestige in this

new position was on the warpath, so Hawk longed
for battle, and his deepest wish was for Stabs-The-
Bear to be well again so that he could become a
Strong Heart, too.

In the midst of his delirium Stabs-The-Bear voiced
things which Standing Elk, the *shaman*, knew to be
whisperings from the spirit land. This might mean
that the boy was dying, or it might mean that Stabs-
The-Bear was of the true far-seers, or both these
things. But the very possibility that here was one
who might carry the vision for his people made
Standing Elk surpass himself as a healer. By the seventh day he knew that the deathly sickness was de-
feated and the boy would live. The *shaman* knew
something more: the flesh would heal but the injury
to the bone would make Stabs-The-Bear lame for
life. To one like Hawk such a handicap would be
worse than death, but for this one, if he sensed true,
lameness might save him for the medicine path, the
priesthood.

Just as Standing Elk had not been altogether happy over Hawk's first kill, so now he could not be altogether sad about this thing which might well make
Stabs-The-Bear his disciple. But when Hawk learned
that his brother would be crippled for life he stripped

himself of all adornment, including the two eagle feathers of valor in his hair. Dressed only in an old leather breech-clout he sat wailing formally outside the tipi. Some of his new friends among the Strong Hearts stood watching, and, understanding his grief, they wailed with him.

CHAPTER SEVEN

Sitting Bull

WORD HAD COME to the Oglala under Horned Thunder that a great event was to take place at Standing Rock, namely the choosing of one head chief for all the Teton Sioux. This was because the old system of many chiefs had led to trouble and disagreement, particularly in dealing with the white men, and there was great need for the tribes to think and to fight together.

Ever since the Sand Creek Massacre of 1865, four years ago, there had been red destruction through all the country of the Sioux. The year that followed was called The-Bloody-Year-Upon-The-Plains. Sioux drums sounded through the nights, smoke signals

97

rose through the days in great white puffs, and mirrors flashed from hill to hill as the people told each other of battles that had been and battles to come, of treaties made by the whites and then broken by the whites at their own convenience. In that year also the white men had cut a road straight through the Sioux's best hunting ground near the Bighorn Mountains, which Government had promised would always be Sioux territory. Now there was a new treaty promising the Sioux the Black Hills and the Powder River Country. But by this time the Indians believed nothing the white men said.

Today the Oglala were striking camp for the journey to Standing Rock. Already in the early morning the squaws were loading the *travois*. As the cavalcade got under way the young warriors paraded along the flanks of the column, each riding his best war horse and wearing full paint and eagle plumes. The long lances they carried had eagle feathers fastened to the shafts. The warriors were singing Strong Heart songs. Hawk rode with them on Cetan, carrying his old Sharps rifle and singing especially loud and clear when the song was one of Sitting Bull's own:

Comrades, whoever runs away,
He is a woman, they say;
Therefore, through many trials,
My life is short!

Hawk missed his brother, Stabs-The-Bear, who was riding with the older men at the center of the company. Since he had been delivered of the fever demons, Stabs-The-Bear had seemed happiest in the company of the foster father whose powerful medicine had healed him of his wounds. Hawk knew that his brother's heart was still one with his own, but it was clear to him that their paths of life now forked. Hawk knew also that their father had wished for a son who would follow him in the priestly way. So, though he had lost his closest companion, Hawk was glad for his father, for now he had that son. Stabs-The-Bear's lameness was a secret grief to him, but as Standing Elk had said, the body's loss might well be the spirit's gain.

To the *shaman*, Stabs-The-Bear had become helper as well as pupil. If there was illness or other trouble in the tribe, Stabs-The-Bear was at his side listening and assisting with it all. And on occasion when the *shaman's* mind darkened with concern for his people and his powers seemed to flag, the faith of his foster son restored his own.

There was need of faith in these troubled days. The white men were greedy and broke all promises. More and more of them were coming into Sioux territory, bringing with them the Gun-That-Goes-On-Shooting, killing the buffalo and the people themselves in ever greater numbers. All knew that the white man meant to take even the Black Hills of Dakota, Sitting Bull's beloved land, for gold had been found there. This would mean great trouble, for Sitting Bull would surely fight for his own.

It was noon of the fourth day when the Oglala sighted the big Sioux encampment. Bands from every tribe of the prairie Sioux were coming in: Minniconjou, Sans Arc, Blackfeet, Brule, Two Kettle, Hunkpapa, also some friendly Cheyennes and Arapahoes. Each tribe had its circle of lodges, and as always each family tipi had its own familiar position in the circle. The Oglala under Chief Crazy Horse were already encamped and Horned Thunder's band joined them. A special council lodge, large as three ordinary tipis, was going up in the middle of the Sioux encampment. Four Horns, Sitting Bull's uncle, nominal head of them all, stood directing the work, and other famous chiefs were passing back and forth among the lodges: Gall and Black Eagle, Loud-Voiced Hawk, Spotted Tail, and Inkpaduta of the Santee Sioux from the east. Hawk and Stabs-The-Bear and other young Oglala men watched from a distance for glimpses of these great ones. Once, just within a lodge opening, they saw the ash-smeared visage of Looks-To-An-Owl, the feared Sans Arc medicine priest, a man of such power, it was rumored, that he could send forth a thought so evil that it would strike a warrior down. But especially was Hawk watching for Sitting Bull, who might appear at any time.

As soon as Willow Woman and Wood Mouse had set up the tipi, Standing Elk entered alone to commune with the spirits of the place and the time. He must be present tonight in the Council Lodge when the chiefs and head men made the final decision as to who would be made chief of all the Sioux. And tomorrow there would be a great meeting in the Council Lodge and he among others would be asked to speak. He must know well his heart in many matters in order to speak truly.

The *shaman* sat silently with his medicine bundle, in deep thought.

Here were his people arrayed in great power, but all was not well. The recent murder of Bear Ribs, the "paper chief" of the Sioux, named so by the whites but killed by two of his own men, was a shame upon them all. This was an indication and a warning of what came from truckling to the white men. Bear Ribs had been persuaded to accept monthly payment from Government for renouncing the war path. But what man could renounce the war path for his people when everywhere there were broken treaties and cheating traders and bloodshed? The Santee of Minnesota had been driven to madness by lies and treachery and had slaughtered many white men before fleeing the land of their fathers, and now the whole Sioux Nation was blamed for the Santee rebellion.

At this meeting were Spotted Tail, the Brule chief, and Red Cloud, highest chief of the Oglala, both ready to sign more treaties with the white men. But all promises made would be broken in this time of great hate. Sitting Bull had said: "Make friends with the white man and if his soldiers do not kill you the hostiles of your own people will." Sitting Bull knew. He was a great warrior, but he was a wise *shaman* as well. In silence Standing Elk put forth a strong prayer that Sitting Bull would be the man chosen at this meeting.

In the Council Lodge that night Standing Elk sat in the background listening and at times praying while the chiefs smoked and spoke in their turn, extolling the deeds and war records of those few who were being considered. Growing upon Standing Elk was a strong sense that all were in accord, including Four Horns himself. Truly the choice was made before the formalities of choosing had begun. Such agreement was good. But nothing could hasten the process of eulogizing and recounting which was a solemn part of any council, and time-honored custom.

Next morning dawned fine and bright, a good omen, Standing Elk thought. When the sun appeared above the river trees a delegation of four chiefs emerged from the Council Lodge. These were Four Horns himself, Loud-Voiced Hawk, Red Horn, and Running Antelope. Standing Elk watched the chiefs take up the buffalo robe for the ceremony which was to follow. The entire village stood waiting and watching, as if none had slept, for never before had one man been chosen as chief over all Sioux tribes. In solemn procession the four walked down the aisle between the lodges, Standing Elk and others of the elders following after.

An audible breath like a great sigh came from the watchers. The four chiefs had stopped before the tipi of Sitting Bull, who was called forth. Spreading the robe flat on the ground, Four Horns asked his nephew to be seated upon it. Now each of the four took a corner of the robe, lifting Sitting Bull. Slowly and solemnly they carried him back to the Council Lodge. If Sitting Bull had had any expectation of this great honor, surely he had not dressed for the occasion. He was wearing a plain buckskin shirt and there were only two eagle feathers in his hair, one of them red in remembrance of recent wounds. His manner, Standing Elk saw with a glow of heart, was as humble as his dress. But on the broad, strong face, as always, were the lines of a smile-about-to-come-out. Instead of being carried by chiefs upon the robe of honor he might have been sitting his own pony on a casual ride in the hills.

Back in the Council Lodge Sitting Bull was given the place of honor and the long pipe was lighted to signify the beginning of the ceremonies. Four Horns, the first to smoke it, pointed the mouthpiece toward the earth for strength and to bind all as brothers, then to the four quarters of the compass, that none of the four winds should blow ill, and last to the sun for true vision. Now the pipe was passed from right to left, around the circle of which Standing Elk was a part. With each exhale a prayer was breathed to *Wahkan-Tanka,* the Great One. Tied to the long pipe were duck feathers which shed water and wind alike, symbolizing the same qualities in the chosen chief, for this pipe was the badge of office and would henceforth belong to Sitting Bull.

At last Four Horns stood up and addressed Sitting Bull.

"Because of your bravery on the battlefield and your reputation as the bravest warrior among us, we have elected you Head Chief of the entire Sioux Nation, Head War Chief. It is your duty to see that the people are fed, that they have plenty. When you say 'fight' we shall fight; when you say 'make peace' we shall make peace."

Now began the tales of the new chief's bravery in battle, of his generosity, and his many *coups.* In his turn Standing Elk rose to say that his heart, long burdened by concern for his people, was now eased, for in Sitting Bull kindness and bravery were equal and even mercy was there for captives and animals.

Only a man of great heart who was also a great warrior could lead the people now, Standing Elk said, for there were times when peace was the bravest way, the only way, and such a time was ahead for all of them.

"Think of *Wahkan-Tanka* and pray well," the *shaman* ended. "For without the Great One our power is nothing. Be like the eagle, the chief of all birds, who flies highest, whose feathers are the reward of valor."

Afterwards a crown was placed on the head of Sitting Bull, a splendid war bonnet of black and white eagle plumes, with a double tail of feathers which hung down the back to the ground. Each feather represented the brave deed or *coup* of the warrior who gave it, for this head-dress symbolized the acts of courage of the whole Sioux Nation. Other presents were a bow and ten arrows and a Hawkens rifle. Also a fine white horse that awaited him at the lodge opening.

When the meeting ended, two chiefs lifted Sitting Bull into the saddle. The Strong Hearts and other warrior societies rode behind him with deerskin shirts stained red and yellow, and decorated with human hair, porcupine quills, and colored beads. They carried their lances and shields, and their horses were painted as for war.

As the procession passed around the great camp circle of the crowded Sioux encampment, the new chief broke into impromptu song:

> *Ye tribes, behold me!*
> *The chiefs of old are gone.*
> *Myself, I shall take courage.*

"*Hau, hau, hau!*" came the booming response from the young warriors.

Hawk was among these, conscious that this was the proudest moment of his life. The words and the voice of Sitting Bull filled him like liquid fire. Here was a chief who bore the charmed life to which every warrior aspired. Surely success would be theirs now that they rode with this one!

CHAPTER EIGHT

The Iron Monster

IN A DOZEN or more sandy wallows along the Yellowstone two and three-year-old bulls were trying out their strength and skill in the bright spring sunlight. Some of them had been at it for hours and had sunk to their knees in exhaustion, horns still engaged, strings of froth hanging from their muzzles. None of this fighting was lethal, none of them knew quite what he was fighting about, but it was a very serious matter nonetheless. Kahtanka had worsted three rivals, one of them a three-year-old. He was trembling from exertion, but preparing to take on a fourth contestant when something in his imperious challenge brought a six-year-old bull down on him.

Kahtanka was overpowered and driven a hundred yards or so into a dense thicket of chokecherry before the older bull forgot him to take a bath.

In a nearby glade his adopted sister was feeding with some other females. Though more than half-grown, she was still a focal point of attention to the numerous cows that had mothered her. Beaverskin saw him at once and gave a friendly bawl of greeting, but there was no longer any place for females in the new male world into which Kahtanka had grown. He pivoted about with a bellow of disgust and crashed away through the thickets. Once in the open he lowered to his knees and took out the remainder of his combativeness tearing up the earth with his short black horns.

Afterwards Kahtanka sought out his hero once more, the master of the herd. More and more of late he had watched and studied the leader. This afternoon Kahtanka found his sire standing near a mud wallow in which he had lain for an hour. Now he was almost completely coated with drying mud, an armor against the flies as well as cooling to the wrath which had never left him since the first terrible slaughter on the Rio Grande. Not even these peaceful weeks on the Yellowstone had released the herd master from the prolonged fury that was consuming him. The great new threat to his race he felt in every atom of his being, and the dark knowledge of what awaited them along the old southern trails was always with him. His preoccupation with this wrapped him in a red mist of brooding so that he was often oblivious to present herd affairs and even present dangers.

The herd leader looked almost lifeless today, a mud monster of utter stillness. But as Kahtanka watched there came a windy blast from his flaring black nostrils that lifted puffs of sandy dust beneath his forefeet. In the matted tangle of his wool an eye rolled whitely. Even in repose there was a glare in that eye to make a spike bull quail, but Kahtanka held his ground. Now he became as moveless as his sire, head also low and eyes inturned with brooding, for what he sensed here was a storm to still his own small tempest. He seemed to tune in to an overall feeling with his sire so that for a space the wrath and worry of the herd master were almost his own, and the urge was in him to share some responsibility never before sensed.

Soon this feeling was interrupted by a stirring in the nearby shadows. Partly screened in leaves was the lowered head and hump of the big reddish bull that seemed always to be watching the herd master. He must have been there all the time, for there had been no movement or sound of his coming. Numerous times before Kahtanka had seen him thus, his measuring gaze fixed on the old leader. Vague threat was in it. Kahtanka's neck bristled, but the herd master seemed quite unaware. Kahtanka voiced a low bellow, not at The Watcher, but hoping somehow to rouse his sire. The white eye rolled once, but the great head did not turn. Kahtanka moved forward and bawled again. What happened then was that the herd master wheeled on him with downwhipped head and Kahtanka found himself fleeing for his very life.

As the summer advanced, The Watcher was officiously to the fore among the younger bulls, usurping special feeding grounds and mud wallows, starting fights, always acting as a separative influence. He kept a constant eye on the herd master, usually from a screen of young trees or dense thicket, and as the rutting season approached he watched the leader's cows as well. Of this particular watching the old sire was well aware, though he appeared regally oblivious.

SEPTEMBER had come again and fox grapes and wild plums were ripe along the Milk River. Kahtanka, now in his fourth year, was seething with new urges to try out his strength and find his own place in the herd. Almost overnight he had become very interested in his foster sister, Beaverskin, while she, strangely enough, had become coy and capricious and no longer sisterly at all. In fact she seemed bent on eluding him and was often seen in the company of one or another young males, almost as if she preferred their company to his. It kept Kahtanka worn thin keeping tab on her and fighting any and all young bulls who got in his way.

These battles were getting more and more serious. Mostly Kahtanka won, but at times he was driven to his very knees in exhaustion before his opponent gave over or was put to rout. Even now, as he turned from his sketchy feeding, Beaverskin was out of sight again, and he moved rapidly along her trail, blasting out a loud challenge as he went. Before he had caught sight of her he was brought up sharp by a sod-shaking rumble from a nearby hill, rumor of a battle being joined, a battle of such magnitude that it behooved him to go and see. He wheeled and hurried toward the commotion.

At last his sire and The Watcher had come together with a crash of lowered heads. Forehead to
forehead, eyes glaring only a foot apart, they heaved
and struggled, breath rasping hoarsely, the muscles
of their necks and shoulders strained to cracking.
Like Kahtanka, numerous other young bulls were
drawing in to watch, stamping and blasting in reflex
excitement. In fact the only movement for a time
was in the ringside, for the matched strength of the
fighters kept them almost stationary. As the tension
mounted the onlookers shifted and pawed the earth
excitedly so that clots of loam went flying into the
air.

For Kahtanka there was much more in this conflict than the mere reflex of battle, for at last his sire
was attending to The Watcher, something he had
long been quivering to see come to pass. From the
first Kahtanka had been aware that The Watcher
wanted to take his sire's place. It rankled him to see
this would-be usurper assuming authority and always watching for some dark hour of which he could
take lethal advantage. Why his sire had not killed
The Watcher outright he could not understand.
Now at last they were fighting, and though for a
moment the power of the battlers seemed balanced

there was no least question as to who would win.
Each low-thrusting head was boulder firm, meeting
each slightest shift of the other's neck and shoulder
muscles as they sparred subtly for an inch or two
of give or gain and did not find even that.

At the outset The Watcher had seized the advantage of the uphill position. Even so, by almost im-
perceptible degrees there came a change. In The
Watcher there was a quiver which Kahtanka could
feel in all his blood and fibers, having lived all these
moments in his own battles. The quiver became a
jerk. Abruptly now the herd master underran his opponent, lifted and hung him high on his horns. This
could end in swift evisceration and a bloody death,
and this Kahtanka counted on. But it did not happen. After a brief moment in which he proved himself victor, the herd master simply tossed the bawling bulk of his would-be rival aside. The Watcher
climbed up out of the dust and without even a look
behind him plunged away among the trees.

Through the circle of younger bulls ran an invol-
untary bellowing of released tension. A day would
come when the old king would inevitably be overthrown, but it was not yet. The herd master had tri-
umphed, although he had not followed up his vic-

tory; he had merely turned back to his waiting cows. Kahtanka was filled with amazement, then with frustration, at the outcome of the battle. In the midst of growing anger his own concern reasserted itself, namely Beaverskin. Where was she now?

He plunged riverward through alder and willow. As he went a roar started somewhere in the depths of him, a lion-like roar of total assertion that startled Kahtanka himself even more than the surrounding herd. At a bend of the river he burst in full view of Beaverskin and her usual group of admirers. This time he did not even need to fight. His imperious bellowing cleared the glade of rivals in short order. Beaverskin, for her part, seemed in no mood to run away. It was as if she had been waiting for this moment. Hadn't she always belonged to Kahtanka anyhow?

ONCE WON, Beaverskin was the old familiar and faithful companion. Kahtanka's battles continued as a matter of course, for the victor must guard and hold his spoils, and add to them when possible. But Beaverskin was first with Kahtanka and he guarded her closely, not only against other bulls and the preyers of the wild, but against hunters, too, whether with silent arrow or crashing gun. It seemed he was continually thrusting his body between her and danger.

The herd had been later this year in leaving the Yellowstone and the first flurries of snow powdered the coats of the moving legion. Before they reached the Moreau River the storm had turned into a blizzard. The bison faced straight into it as was their wont for their heavily wooled heads and fore quarters were all but proof against the weather. For three days, while the storm raged, they moved slowly north and west, off their usual course. When the wind dropped they headed south as before.

At the juncture of the Grand and Missouri Rivers, where wagon trains stopped on the western trail, no herd could pass without drawing an organized attack. Making new trails was against every instinct of the bison kind and at this particular point the old ways were cut two feet deep into the prairie soil, drawing their feet like grooves. Even so, the leaders had learned to fear this spot. This fall the herd made a wider circle than ever before, only to be brought up short by a thing unknowable and frightening beyond belief. For across the plain, stretching east and west into the far distance, ran two shining bands of steel dividing north from south.

The leaders halted the herd. A great new threat lay here, for the scent of man was mingled with other strange scents. The herd hung at pause, all heads turned toward the ominous barrier, waiting for the nature of the threat to reveal itself. As nothing happened, the leading bulls, nonplussed, became restive and wrathful. Abruptly a small band under an old bull that had joined the main herd in Montana crossed the tracks and surged away southward and out of sight. But the main movement of the big herd was back and away from the rails.

To the herd master this barrier was a final affront. Man, having pursued his kind relentlessly, slaughtering more and more, was now blocking the very path of the herd. This could not be tolerated. He was ready to battle anything, if only there was something to fight.

Hours passed before the sound came, at first faint, a humming vibration that came from the steel barrier itself, now glaring bright in the afternoon sun. Clearly this was a warning. The rails were like somnolent snakes awakening to life. Parts of the herd rolled back, but the old leader moved forward rumbling. The warning sound gradually increased. Finally out from the eastern hills along the shining bands came a great thing snorting and blowing like a monster bull and finally sounding a whistling blast of challenge. Smoke rose above it like a thrown-up dust cloud and the very ground trembled.

Something to fight at last, a very Minotaur. Fear was not in the old master, except for his herd. Now he was a seething core of wrath that welcomed this tangible opposition. His peremptory bellow mustered the leading bulls and flung them forward, himself in the forefront, in a head-on charge straight at the fuming monster.

At sight of the buffalo herd ahead, the engineer had prudently slowed the train almost to a stop in the hope of avoiding trouble. On this recently opened line of the Union Pacific, trains had been known to be delayed for hours, or even derailed, by far fewer bison than now confronted him. He sounded his whistle continuously and loosed blasts of steam in the hope of startling the animals away, but without success. As the drive-wheels slowed to a near stop he saw a huge black bull break into full charge straight at the locomotive.

The impact flung both the engineer and his fireman forward against the fire-box. The engine heaved, swayed, and left the rails, almost toppling over. Above the thunder of countless hoofs came a crashing and splintering of cars behind, followed by the screams and shouts of panicked passengers. Above the tumult rifles began to roar as hunters among the passengers took over. Even so there were precarious minutes of pressing and scraping of horns and shaggy bodies against the trainside. Two cars were all but capsized before the riflemen succeeded in splitting and turning the tide.

For the big black bull that had started it all it had been a suicidal charge. The herd master's massive body lay beside the track, his shattered skull wedged beneath the wheels of the monster he had all but overthrown.

T H E   H E R D lingered on in Dakota Territory that fall, partly because the customary southern route was blocked by the railroad which they would not cross, partly because authority had been dangerously divided since the death of the old herd master.

Leadership was a three-way matter now, between a huge old grandfather bull whose remaining authority was merely a matter of size and weight, The Watcher, the most logical contestant for kingship, and Kahtanka himself, who was of the master breed, though still young. The three bulls balanced each other in influence, but continually offset each other in effect, so that the herd was divided into three separate parts and much of the sagacity that should have gone into wariness and herd government was spent in watchful enmity. Even when the bison were beset once more by hide hunters on the Red River there was a confusion of issues that played into the enemy's hands.

By the death of the herd master The Watcher had gained his most desired end without danger or cost to himself. His main obstacle to general herd priority was out of the way, but there remained the two other contestants. The grandfather bull could be overthrown; there were a number of ways to accomplish this. Kahtanka would have to be contended with more directly. The Watcher's first concern was the old titan, now the figurehead of power in the herd.

There were numerous other bulls who seconded

The Watcher's every move and idea, natural admirers of power and influence and watchers in their turn. The time had come, The Watcher sensed, to put these supporters to use. Old as he was, the grandfather bull was too mighty to be engaged outright without risk. The Watcher counted on firing his clique of admirers to the point where they would back him in a lethal attack. On the day The Watcher chose for the overthrow of the old one there were five of them at his back. With no warning whatever The Watcher charged like a catapult into the old one's unprotected shoulder. His summoning bellow brought a concerted attack from the younger bulls which cut out the patriarch from the midst of his clan and began the long, cruel game of harrying him out of the herd.

Led by The Watcher, all through that afternoon the young guard, singly and in pairs, kept up the attack on the old one, wearing him down, not even letting him feed. By nightfall he was completely cut off from his cows, but because of his size and weight no definite conclusion had been reached. Bloody and ragged of hide, too tough to kill, it seemed, the old bull had still the rugged resistance of a great tree. He was a true patriarch, the great-great-grandfather of scores of buffalo in the herd, including some of his attackers.

Not even at night did they let him rest, for other young bulls were joining in this ousting of the old one, activated by the craving for priority in herd affairs. By the next mid-day the old one had been driven afar on the plain, thrust out and kept moving away. The grandfather bull understood now and accepted his fate; henceforth he was to be an outcast, a lone one, forbidden to return to the herd. It was the fate of many a patriarch. He himself in the insecurity of youth had also banded against aged bulls and driven them forth to conclude their days in solitude.

It was nightfall when The Watcher rejoined the herd, followed by his clique, blasting and bugling importantly, his chesty bellow echoed by his followers. Insolence and insubordination was in every sound and movement of them all. Sudden anger whipped Kahtanka, the wrath of a monarch, instantaneous and terrible. As The Watcher came up at a ponderous trot, blaring as in challenge, Kahtanka moved suddenly out from his own band and crashed into the other's shoulder with a lifting twist of head and horns. The impact jolted The Watcher and flung him violently sidewise. He was stopped and silenced, his confidence jarred. For a moment the two bulls glared at each other while their enmity deepened. Both knew that a lethal clash was building between them. But the time was not yet, for The Watcher suddenly swung aside and moved away among his cohorts.

CHAPTER NINE

Stampede

THE FOLLOWING year, as never before, the white-topped caravans of the settlers dotted the northern plains and hide hunters and their wagons lurked in the canyons and among the trees of the river bottoms as the herd moved southward.

The great need now was for the sensing of threat where no threat appeared to be, or ever was before. Change of direction or change of pace or both might be demanded at any moment for very life's sake. Of the several possible herd leaders, Kahtanka's vigilance was the keenest and most constant. Numerous times in the past year he had been forewarned by some instinct and had shifted the course of travel in

time to avert a waiting menace. This added awareness made him nominal head of a large portion of
the herd, though true herd leadership had yet to be
established.

As usual, smaller bands of buffalo that had summered apart joined the big herd as it moved south
from the Yellowstone. October was warm this year
and the herd had lingered overlong in this broad
side valley of the Shoshone, where high rocky bluffs
on either side protected them from surprise attack
and the sun-cured buffalo grass made rich feeding.

It was here that the Corning party of hide hunters
caught up with the herd. For two days they dogged
the herd, making stand after stand with their im-
proved 50-caliber repeating rifles, more than ever
effective now. Once again the plain was strewn with
skinned carcasses and the sky was dark with carrion
birds.

Throughout the attacks Kahtanka's chief concern
had been the protection of Beaverskin and his immediate clan. On the second afternoon, when a
mounted hunter actually singled them out, Kahtanka kept cutting between the hunter and Beaverskin and succeeded in herding her to safety in the
thick of numbers.

THAT EVENING in the camp of the hide hunters, Joe Riopelle sat on a bale of hides nursing a tin cup between his hands. He was exhausted from the hard-riding hunt which had lasted since the first gray streaks of dawn, yet filled with a sense of tension which his twenty-five years in the open had taught him to heed. Riopelle was the guide and scout of the Corning party. He had a one-third interest in the hide project, the money for which was being put up by the easterner, Jules Corning. Corning was a big-game hunter who knew nothing about this country except that there was great profit in buffalo hides, and he was out after it.

Johnson, the head skinner, was just coming in with a wagon loaded with fresh hides. Out on the valley floor eight other men were at work in the last light, girdling and stripping the fresh-killed carcasses with swift practiced strokes of their knives. Already the big carrion birds had come in. They sat in waiting rows flexing their wings and making their peculiar retching sounds in anticipation, then flapping in to claim the carcasses as the skinners moved away.

Riopelle took his slice of buffalo hump off the fire and put another on for Johnson. Corning had not even stopped for coffee, but had ridden away with two fresh rifles, hoping for a final stand before dark.

"Did he say anything?" Johnson asked as he came up.

"Talked about a young cow he'd sighted with a coat like silk. Sounded like a beaver-robe. Anyhow he's hell-bent to get her."

"After a day like this!" Johnson snorted. "I figured it was beginning to get him. Thanks," he added, as Riopelle forked his piece of seared meat onto a plate and handed it to him.

"I told him this morning we had a capacity load already and ought to head back to Laramie. Snapped at me like a feist. Said he'd organized this outfit for action, he was paying for it, and was going to get it. He's liable to get more than he's paying for, hanging on in Sioux territory like this. I should never have let him talk me into bringing him here."

"They're talking about us right now," Johnson said, motioning toward a far pencil of smoke beyond the bluffs to the west.

Riopelle nodded. "They know every move we make. That's why I let him camp out in the open like this. Like I told him, they'll likely let us be for twenty-four hours or so; after that no telling. Reminded him we had a treaty with the Sioux to keep out of their hunting ground. He just laughed. 'I carry my own treaty right *here*,' he told me, and he tapped his rifle. I don't like him. Know how he made his biggest stand this morning—two of 'em, in fact? Shot a calf, careful just to wound it, so its bawling would make its mother and the rest of its clan turn back the way they do. He just waited there and shot the lot! Not that I'm soft or anything, but that sort of thing shows a man up. I knew what he was before we started. I've seen the type before. Should never have taken the job!"

Johnson's tired gaze had been focussed on Riopelle as he spoke. Abruptly he flung his half-eaten meat into the fire. "Joe, I'm sick of it all! Sick of the bulls! Nobody knows! I'll tell you something; this is my last trip as a skinner, so help me!"

"Glad to say it's my last trip for the year," Riopelle said.

It was long past dark and the men were in their blankets when Corning rode in. He merely dropped the reins over the neck of his lathered horse, sat down on a pile of hides in the firelight, and began a meticulous cleaning of his two guns. Joe Riopelle had beans, meat and coffee ready but he left the fire to unsaddle and rub down Corning's overheated mount.

"How about some feed and water for me?" Corning asked.

"You might want to use that horse another time," Riopelle said. "He's about blowed and this wind's veered north." He came back to the fire and filled Corning's cup and plate. "You must have run that silk-robe cow clear out of the country," he added.

"I sighted her twice, not more than a hundred yards away, but the damned bulls kept milling in between. One big black fellow seemed to be squiring her and kept cutting in like some special bodyguard. Three or four more hours, though, and I'll get both of 'em. That cow's a prize worth the whole trip."

Riopelle let the man eat and drain his second cup of coffee before he said: "You've stayed twenty-four hours over the promised time in here. It's not a healthy spot—Sioux territory like I told you—and all afternoon they've been signaling about us in smoke talk. I advise pulling out at dawn."

"You do, hey? Well, not till I get that cow. *Not under any condition will I leave till I get that beaver-robe cow!*"

FOUR MILES away a band of Oglala fighting men were whetting themselves for battle. Hawk was among them, one of the most zealous of the twenty warriors under White Antelope, who were to attack the hide hunters' camp at dawn. Because of the treaty signed the year before between Sioux and white, Horned Thunder had delayed the attack for forty-eight hours. By the terms of the treaty, white men promised to come through Sioux territory by the Missouri and the White Rivers only, in boats. But these white men had come overland with their wagons. And by moccasin telegraph and smoke signal, word had been coming in of other hide hunters in Sioux country, from the Milk River clear down to the Ree. The plain was covered with their butchery.

In the eyes of the Sioux such hunters were as much the enemy as those who brought war. As Sitting Bull had said at a meeting of the tribal chiefs, the Blue Coats *wanted* their hide hunters to kill and kill! So did all white men, for to kill off the buffalo was the surest way to starve the Indian and force him into the agencies. It was all a great trick and the Sioux must fight.

In the firelight before White Antelope's lodge the twenty chosen warriors stamped and spurned the ground in the rhythm of the battle chant. Prayers had already been sent to the sun and moon, and earthpower was flowing into them, all possible fear banished. In spirit they were unified and focussed, with the strength of many. They were ready, each man alone was ready to face all the enemy. Only waiting was hard now. Cries sounded intermittently as one or another of them voiced the power rising within. There was the eagle scream, the wolf note, the coyote kill-cry. Hawk's was the high skirling of his name-bird, poised for the stoop, and tonight it came from him like a feathered spear from the hand of a victor. If only they could start now, he was thinking, as he wove and bent to the quickening pulse of the drum. But the old men said to wait and rest and rise before the dawn.

It was very late when the young men agreed to separate for the night. In his own tipi the open flap caught the pulsing light of a low fire. Coals, Hawk thought, for the rest would surely be asleep. But in the flickering light, wrapped in their blankets, sat his father and his brother, Stabs-The-Bear. As they turned to him their two faces were as though cut from the same gray stone. Some of Hawk's high fire fell earthward, for here was warning; his heart knew before either had spoken. They waited, smoking, until he had sunk into their stillness. When they spoke, it was as though voicing one man's thoughts.

"There is great evil in the camp of these white men," Standing Elk said. "They are mad weasels. *Wahkan-Tanka* will protect his own, but there will be much death in the dawn."

Stabs-The-Bear added, "Remember, my brother, a fast horse is for running off as well as for running in."

Standing Elk smoked another interval in silence. "Louder than the war songs of the Strong Hearts tonight, for ears that could hear, was the sound of the *pahaiyaane*, the voices of the dead."

"When there is great evil," Hawk replied after a space, "there is the need to kill."

"You have fought the Crow, you have fought the Cheyenne," Standing Elk told him. "Like smoke. Now you fight the fire itself."

Stabs-The-Bear said, "Last night I dreamed of my father. He called to me and I went to his place, but I was not I. I was my brother, Hawk."

Hawk said nothing, but cold ran over his skin. He knew these dreams of his brother, and this one was very clear.

THEY APPROACHED the white man's camp before dawn broke above the eastern bluffs. The hide hunters were not all asleep. A small fire glowed in the dimness and around it the horses and wagons were drawn up in a circle, as though forewarned. Even as the braves swept forward with their first war cries, shots came from behind the wagons and Pretty Weasel clung dying to the side of his horse as they veered away.

The war party circled in the dimness. Hawk's horse snorted and turned violently from a skinned and bloody carcass lying on the nearby flats. A coyote scutted away from it. Once more the braves swept in at full gallop but were met with such a withering fire that they were obliged to veer aside and speed out of gunshot.

One of the warriors had a charm: he had long lived with a ghost which protected him from all harm. As the dawn light began to break over them, Lives-With-A-Ghost spoke to White Antelope.

"I will ride in now and find out how many there are of them and let them empty their guns," he said.

White Antelope nodded agreement.

Sitting erect, Lives-With-A-Ghost pressed his horse to a gallop straight toward the clustered wagons. The waiting braves saw him ride the length of the camp with guns spitting red in the dim light, saw him wheel and start back. Then the hoofbeats ended as horse and rider went down, and there was silence. They waited now for Lives-With-A-Ghost to rise and return on foot, for horses had been shot from under him before this. But there was no further sound or movement.

If Lives-With-A-Ghost could be killed or even wounded by these mad weasels it was the worst of signs. But not a man of them suggested that they withdraw.

"We should have charged straight in at the start," White Antelope said. "Now they are all awake and have many guns."

"We must charge now!" said Hurries-To-War. "*Hopo! Hopo!* Let's go!"

There were *hau's* of approval.

"Ride fast. Turn aside for nothing," White Antelope instructed. He assigned Many Horses to find the body of Lives-With-A-Ghost and bring him out.

The running charge was met by another blast of rifle fire. Strong Hearts on either side of Hawk went down. Hawk got in a single shot with his Sharps rifle but could not know if it had told. He heard the report of the other three Oglala guns. But in the white man's fire there was no break at all; the bullets kept coming like hail. Hawk had his bow and whipped an arrow to the thong, but never drew it taut because in that instant a bullet caught him in the side, almost spinning him off his horse. He dropped forward on Cetan's neck while the animal swerved to the right and went streaking away.

In near-unconsciousness Hawk heard again the words of his brother: "A fast horse is for running off as well as for running in."

He awoke from a little death, still somehow clinging to Cetan's mane, to find White Antelope and Iron Dog riding close beside him. Hawk made out six other warriors in the morning light, among them Many Horses with the body of Lives-With-A-Ghost before him, lying across the neck of his mount. The fighting was over, and Hawk knew without being told that they had left eleven of their twenty behind.

Chief Horned Thunder heard the story in the council lodge. White Antelope urged that a large company of fighting men surround the interlopers, even conduct a prolonged siege, if necessary, cutting off the white mens' water supply, and starving them out.

Horned Thunder weighed this, but said, "Standing Elk will first make medicine."

The *shaman*, with Stabs-The-Bear, was working over Hawk when the war chief and a delegation of fighting men came to his tipi.

"I have already made medicine," Standing Elk said. "A plan has been shown. What is to be done must be done swiftly."

The *shaman* outlined the plan which had come from *Wahkan-Tanka*, the Great One. As he talked, many hands lifted to cover mouths in gestures of awe and grim appreciation.

"If Horned Thunder gives the word I myself will lead the way," the *shaman* said.

Horned Thunder was not only in agreement with the plan, but himself would ride with Standing Elk. Before the sun was more than two hours high, tipis were furled, goods piled on *travois*, and the entire camp was moving toward the hills.

The very breeze was right.

JOHNSON, the head skinner, looked around from his baling of hides. "Listen to that!" he said.

"I have been," said Joe Riopelle.

"Thought it was thunder at first but there's not a cloud in sight. Do you know what it is?" Johnson asked.

"Buffalo on the move!"

Pfaff and Jenson, two other skinners, stood by listening, looking scared.

"Better get on lively with those hides," Riopelle told them, an edge to his voice. He was piling the cooking gear under a wagon seat.

"Think they're heading this way?" Johnson asked.

Riopelle got down and put his ear to the ground. "We'll know for sure after a minute or so," he said. "One thing's certain, it's the worst place we could be—out in this valley between the bluffs."

Johnson and his men began feverishly loading baled hides into the wagons.

"Never mind being neat!" yelled Riopelle. "If there's too many of 'em just leave 'em. Wonder if *he's* got sense enough to know what's up." Riopelle's gaze had picked out the mounted figure of Corning riding campward. In spite of the dawn Indian attack, the boss had ridden out to a rise of ground a quarter of a mile away to try to locate the nearest remnant of the herd. The quick repulse of the Oglala had fired him with new confidence and his orders had been to wait while he carried forward his hunt for the beaverskin cow.

As Corning rode in he saw Riopelle and two of the other men hastily inspanning the teams. "What's all this?" he demanded.

"Haven't you *heard?*" Riopelle said tensely. "It's getting louder, you notice. The way I figure we've got about fifteen minutes to get off this valley floor where we never should have been in the first place. That's a buffalo stampede!"

"How do you know they're headed this way?" Corning said.

"Listen! Louder every minute!"

"No way of telling they're coming straight through here," Corning argued.

"They're in this valley! Where else is there for them to go?"

"There may be branch valleys—"

"There aren't!" Riopelle said flatly. "This is an old river bed, and those red devils know it." He pointed to a rising cloud of smoke far down the valley. "Sioux work, you can depend on that—"

Corning was still stubborn. "What's the matter with backing wagons up in a big V and getting behind with our guns. We could shoot them as they come and pile up a bulwark."

"Not this time! You're listening to half a million buffalo coming at full speed! Nothing but boulders would split that rush!"

Not a man had paused in his work during this exchange, and now two wagons were loaded and ready. Riopelle gave the order to move.

"Head straight for those bluffs and follow them along the valley to the first opening!"

"Look here! I give the orders in this outfit!"

But Corning's words were lost. No one even glanced his way. Two wagons were already creaking and rattling across the flats. The sound of the stampede was louder each moment now. The earth's crust boomed like a fast-beaten drum. Four other wagons swung quickly after the first two, leaving behind the many bales of hides.

Corning loosed a stream of violent protest but Riopelle himself was leaving now in the last of the wagons, lashing the rumps of his team. Ridiculous as this all-out flight on the part of hardened plainsmen seemed to him, Corning now vaulted to the saddle and spurred down-valley.

Riopelle had given them fifteen minutes. Less

than ten had passed when round a distant bend of the valley the first of the buffalo came in sight, a solid-dark shoulder-to-shoulder press filling the valley from bluff to bluff. Off to the left the galloping teams with their clattering, bounding wagons had turned down-valley in what was now a race with death, for so far not even the narrowest break had shown in the rocky walls.

Corning, far ahead on his fast saddle horse, discovered the first break in the rock barrier, a steep, narrow fissure just wide enough for him to force his mount upward some fifteen feet amid loose shale and rock. His winded horse was braced there trembling, on a thirty-degree slant. Corning could not force him farther and he dared not dismount because of the sliding and unsure footing in this narrow defile. To hold the animal steady until the living avalanche had swept past was the most that he could hope for. Over his shoulder he became aware of the wagons passing below, pounding high over rocks and jettisoning their loads, the men barely managing to stay on the high seats. Screams of a terrified horse rose above the din.

Now the pound and throb of the stampede quivered up the very legs of Corning's mount and shud-

dered through the man's body till his teeth rattled
and he had to grind them together to steady his jerk-
ing face. Then the brown-black river of bison was
just below him, even mounting toward him like a
tide, and the hot stench of the surging bodies and
the dull thudding impacts of bone and flesh came
up to him. His horse screamed and reared, white-
eyed, and the loose rocky footing slid from beneath
him. A big rock just above them was loosened by the
slide and horse, man, and rock pitched downward
together. There was one blinding, flashing instant of
seeing on Corning's part before darkness took him.

NOT LONG after the buffalo had passed through
the throat-latch of the valley, spread out, and come
to rest on the plain beside the Shoshone, the Oglala
came riding down along the path of destruction. In
all the valley scarcely a tussock of grass remained
standing; the earth itself was deep bitten by the
countless hoofs. Even the grass fire they had set to
start the stampede had gone out upon reaching the
beaten path of the flight. Near the camp of the white
men the Sioux found the trampled remains of their
own dead who had fallen in the morning attack.

Farther on they saw, over by a narrow opening in the cliff-side, the remains of a man and a horse. But they did not stop just then, for ahead were what was left of the hide wagons: patches of splintered and pulverized wood and a few iron axles and tire rims. Among these were the twisted and broken remains of rifles. Of the white men there was nothing left but formless pulp, not a scalp worth taking as trophy. *Wahkan-Tanka,* the Great One, had completely erased the evil the hunters had brought to this valley. The mad weasels were all dead.

Finally, when the Oglala rode out of the valley mouth onto the river flats they found four of the white men's horses running there, trailing their broken harness. They were very good horses. And on the way back, at the place where the man and the horse had fallen, Stabs-The-Bear's sharp eye picked out one undamaged rifle lodged among the stones in the narrow slot in the cliff-side. There were even bullets in this wonder gun, this prize worth many *coups* to a warrior. It was not for him, for his way led more and more into medicine and magic, but Stabs-The-Bear knew what he would do. He would give the rifle to Hawk, and joy in it would make his brother quickly well.

CHAPTER TEN

King Bull

DOWN ON THE sandy flats of the Shoshone after the stampede, there was a great searching and calling among the spread-out ranks of the bison. The interrelated family bands had become separated and these must draw together again before peace could come to any. Cows, young bulls and calves moved through the ranks, crying for their lost ones. Some of these would never be found, for inevitably many had gone down and been trampled under in the panic flight. Kahtanka and Beaverskin had lost one another and not until nightfall were they reunited, along with others of their clan.

Led by no single bull but by the habit of centuries, the herd was drawn southward and once more approached the railroad. The deepworn trails they knew all led to those shining lines of steel and beyond, winding south along the Missouri. Despite remembered fear of death and the unknown, there was the pull to the south, strong as the very movement of the planet. Kahtanka felt it with the rest, but there was something else that he sensed, too. In the depths of him was the image of his sire, the herd master, head low in long brooding, awaiting the feel of the call. There had always been security in that picture. Where was it now? Now there was not even the old grandfather bull to steady the herd, and there was still strife and dissension among the young usurpers.

Emulating his sire, Kahtanka withdrew to a rise of ground to test the air and await some prompting. Death and danger everywhere was the message that came, so that none of the known ways carried a call. In the midst of his brooding, like part of the memory that had drawn him here, Kahtanka saw dimly a reddish form in the willow wash just below. Partly masked in bushes and waiting as always was The Watcher. Kahtanka pawed the ground and bellowed, but no answering challenge came from the other. Soon the thicket below was empty of the shape of him, and Kahtanka returned to his brooding.

When the buffalo moved forward again it was still southward, toward the crossing where the old herd master had been killed. At the railroad the vanguard of the herd drew up and once more hung at pause in sight of the shining rails. Now there was no puffing, bellowing demon coming along the iron trail, but there was the fearsome smell of it and the scent of man. The warning pressure in Kahtanka increased, a desperate sensing of the need for change without knowing how to bring it about.

Yet somehow the decision was already made in him, for now he was swinging his own following westward and northward, away from the tracks, away from the ancient trails as well. All had been waiting in uncertainty for this token of true authority. Now the secondary bulls and the old leading cows fell in beside Kahtanka in the van, and the entire herd followed, family by family, clan by clan, for without their leaders they were lost. The pivotal turn had been made, the first great migratory change in centuries.

To make sure there would be no turning back,

Kahtanka hazed the flanks and sides of his own clan as well as those that were falling in behind. In his zeal he drove them onward ten full hours without pause, lest the drift toward the south take them over once more. For days thereafter he scarcely slept, his instinct poised like a glass ball in a fountain jet that could never come to rest.

Now none knew from hour to hour what lay over the next rise, or where the next waterholes might be found. Even the feeding was patchy and there were no trails to settle into at their familiar autumn pace. They had lost the old ways and had not yet found a new, and now trepidation instead of peace was multiplied by their very numbers.

Herd movement became sporadic, without the sustained rhythm of the travel lope. This was all against buffalo nature. The magnetic pull southward continued and bull after bull tried to turn his following aside, until chastened by Kahtanka. Even the cowbirds that usually accompanied them deserted the herd after the first freezing nights, all but a few hardy characters who burrowed for warmth into the dense wool of the big bulls' necks and shoulders.

Cold rain and sleet drove down upon these vanguards of a new kind of winter with a grimness such as they had never known before. It drove into their wooly coats and froze in sheaths, so that they crackled as they moved. Then one afternoon the sleet turned into a storm of high-country hail, ice that fell like hurtling stones out of the gray-black sky. Under the bombardment the herd lost all control and broke into short futile flights in one direction after another, flights that were a rebellion against every unfamiliar mile. In the prolonged onslaught of the storm Kahtanka himself lost confidence and simply ran with the rest. But there was no escape, and of one accord they stopped at last, all heads turning into the storm, buffalo-fashion. Now their ice-sheathed coats became an armor of a sort, protection against the terrible hammering from the sky. Even so there was not an animal but was battered and injured. Some of the young had died in the first intense cold. The rest were saved only by huddling beneath their elders. When the storm passed the injured helped each other tongue-dress their wounds. In the intense cold that followed, inches of hailstones remained on the ground, turning their hoofs and making travel most painful.

Westward out of the Dakota ranges into Wyoming the herd moved and here encountered regiments of the south-Canada herd which had crossed the line ahead of the advancing winter. This northern herd was obviously accustomed to wintering here, and if it could subsist so could the newcomers.

When white winter came snarling down upon them, the Canadian herd showed no perturbation, though all forage was covered, and snow and ice locked off the water supply. From the northern bison Kahtanka's herd learned now how to cope with winter: where to paw through the snow for the best forage; how to browse on spruce tips and twigs and the dried berries of the nigrum and cassiope bushes; how to eat snow and lick the ice of the frozen streams for their water; how to huddle in a close mass in the windless ravines so that the heat of their many bodies formed a vapor that hung over them and effectively shielded them from the worst of the cold; and how to use the deep snow itself for protection. It was a matter now of survival of the strong. Many weaklings were weeded out in the first winter weeks and most of the young would have frozen to death had they not been covered at night by the long beards and manes of their elders. The rest became hard and fit beyond anything they had known before.

That winter Kahtanka was at the height of his powers. Two inches over six feet high he was now at his matted hump, and ten feet long, larger by a third than the average bull buffalo, with the in-grained strength of a healthy tooth in all his win-ter-hardened body. Even his usually smooth hind quarters had taken on a short furry coat against the cold. His tufted tail and massive mane gave him a lion-like appearance and his roar of authority carried out the effect. The coarse hair on his forelegs flapped with every step, giving a ponderous dignity to the vast bulk that topped a ton weight by some five hundred pounds.

When the chinooks finally unlocked their forest prison, Kahtanka's herd began drawing eastward at once, leaving their winter friends. There would be other little winters before real spring came but none feared them now.

The spring largesse of feeding more than made up for the rigors of winter. Bunch and deer grass sprang up at the very edge of the receding snow, more succulent than forage they had known. Spike-horn bulls bounded and clashed their forming horns together in an excess of good feeling. And the trees of the vicinity were worn smooth and strung with patches of discarded winter wool where buffalo had rubbed their itching sides and shoulders.

Many calves were dropped that April, a rugged lot, able to travel in a matter of days. In the calving this year there was the usual color assortment—black, brown vari-colored, and buckskin. Also there was one albino, a rarity in any species. Beaverskin produced black bull twins.

On the Yellowstone, in their well-known summer ground, they waited through May and June for old friends and companions of the Dakota and New Mexican herds to join them. Always this had happened here. But this spring none came from the south, nor in the summer months that followed. The great Continental Herd had been permanently divided by the railroad.

Late that summer four white hunters came to the Yellowstone. There was no blood-smell of hide wagons to warn the buffalo this time, for these were trophy hunters who had come north primarily for bear. Although it was still a month before buffalo meat or hides would be prime, the hunters rode down upon the herd one day. They lanced their mounts in among the fleeing buffalo, taking a sportsman's chance to make their kills. Ordinarily these men would have withdrawn after a fast half hour or so, for they were not out after hides. But from a distance one of them had glimpsed the albino calf, a trophy-room prize worth any amount of pursuit.

It was late that day and a third wild chase was on before the hunters brought the white calf down. But by this time one of their number had sighted the light and gleaming coat of Beaverskin, another prize worth the whole of their costly journey in from Denver. The trophy fever was on them and they pressed the hunt until dark, taking several shots at full gallop but without apparent effect because of the shifting ranks. It was several hours before the hunter who had first sighted Beaverskin realized that it was one particular huge black bull that kept shuttling between him and his quarry. It appeared that he would have to bring down the bull if he were ever to bag his prize, so he deliberately placed his next two shots in the bulk of the big black. Then there was a shifting of the bison ranks and a dangerous squeeze around the hunter's own mount. This took all his attention for a space, and both animals were lost to sight. Darkness was already shutting down, the main herd but a diminishing rumble now beyond a bend of the river. In the morning, the hunter decided, he would finish off the black bull, certainly wounded now, and systematically run down the beaver-robe.

That day, in flight after flight, Kahtanka's clan had out-distanced the hunters, but always the pursuit caught up with them again. Desperately he kept driving Beaverskin and the calves to the fore, keeping up a flanking movement in an attempt to shield them in their flight. Once a cow running at Beaverskin's side collapsed and dropped in his path. A little later a yearling just ahead of him suddenly plowed the earth with its muzzle, its body whirling end over end to lie flattened in the wake of the flight. Then something struck Kahtanka, a thudding impact that staggered him. He tried to outrace the fiery burn of it but it would not be left behind.

Once more Kahtanka swerved the flight, interposing his own body as before. That was when the shock and stab of pain struck again, wrenching from him a rumbling challenge as to an enemy. Then the crashing flight dipped into the brush-grown flats and pursuit was lost as night came down.

Too many times now had pursuit been resumed the following day. The only safety lay in far flight. On and on Kahtanka drove his wing of the herd without rest, even though the pain of his wounds was a mounting, dazing torment and he longed only to sink down in the healing mud by the stream bank. By morning the band was twenty miles downstream in a side valley they knew from other years, safe here for a time at least.

The herd fell to browsing, but Kahtanka drew apart. He had lost much blood, and pain and fever almost blinded him, one of the bullets having lodged in the bone above his shoulder. Down by the river he drank and drank, then sought a wallow where he lay with his side half immersed in mud and water. The cool plaster of clay eased his pain and helped draw the poisons from his wounds. Afterward, a vast fearsome effigy of mud, he stood drying and resting beneath the trees. Beaverskin and one of her calves came in the early starshine. She bunted him softly in the flank. He could scarcely move in response, but his plight became plain to her in their soundless communication.

When the mud on his wounds began to crack Kahtanka went back to the wallow, moving with great difficulty. He drank again but did not feed. When night came he was back beneath the trees, sunk down on his unhurt side in a torpor of pain and fatigue in which he would remain until healing or death took over.

Days passed. August had come to an end and the rutting season was at hand. The section of the herd left upriver on the night of the flight had joined Kahtanka's band and the big company of cows that always summered apart began drawing in for the fall running. Everywhere there was stir and uproar, sudden battles, bellows of challenge and mere well-being, for the fires of the mating urge were beginning to sweep the herd. Kahtanka was still deep in lethargy, though healing now and beginning to feed again. His youth and mighty energy and the wine-rare northern air and sunlight were winning the day for him.

One midday he roused from a doze in his favorite shade to see the familiar head and hump of The Watcher above the nearby thickets, in his eye a red and arrogant gleam. When was it that this watching had first begun? Had it ever stopped? Yes, it had stopped for a time after his challenge on the day the grandfather bull had been ousted. That day or any other time, until wounded, Kahtanka could have beaten the other. Now he was weak and ill, as The Watcher well knew, and surveillance had begun

again. It continued the rest of that afternoon. Next
morning it was resumed and now it was not only a
watching of him, as Kahtanka became aware. It in-
cluded Beaverskin and another young cow feeding
in a glade close by.

Abruptly The Watcher surged out of the thickets
into the open, the blare of his purpose quivering the
still air. Up through layers of pain and stiffness and
torpor Kahtanka roused, knowing that the hour so
long pending was at hand and that he had never
been less ready. This must be a fight to the death.
With an answering challenge so deep that it seemed
to come from underground, Kahtanka moved in,
blocking the other's way.

The Watcher wheeled with shaking head, his
pawing forehoofs whipping back and up, flinging
dirt clots above his shoulders. He was a giant in
bulk and length, his sides and humped shoulders one
muscle-packed curve from neck to hips. Through
long waiting his natural belligerence had reached a
lethal point.

Now the two backed off some lengths, bull-fash-
ion, preparatory to a charge. For Kahtanka there
were mists to pierce and crusts of resistance to break
through, for in the last two weeks he had scarcely

moved. Dim-eyed and groggy, he could barely see the form that thundered toward him; he could only strive to meet it head on. In the crash of horn on horn that followed, it was only Kahtanka's great weight which prevented him from being overthrown and laid open to goring at the outset. As it was, the shock of the impact upon his stiffened shoulder muscles rocked him throughout and set him trembling. The second charge came swiftly from the side into the very spot of pain in his wounded shoulder, as if The Watcher knew. Again Kahtanka all but toppled, but the torment roused him and rage came boiling upward, sharpening his reflexes and clearing his sight.

Other bulls were drawing in about the fighters, stamping and blasting in reflex excitement. They knew that all herd affairs hung on this clash. Though Kahtanka had become acknowledged leader in many ways in the past months, The Watcher had also been to the fore in reconnaissance, in courting, in pugnacity, and in general squiring of the herd.

At the third clash their black horns locked and a heaving, groaning trial of strength ensued. The pressure upon his shoulder was so agonizing that Kahtanka kept stumbling on stones and tussocks and had constantly to rewin his balance to even hold his own. The Watcher was forcing him into the downhill position, as in that other battle with his sire. This increased the power of The Watcher's attack, as well as the hazard of Kahtanka's footing. With a pivoting heave of the head The Watcher suddenly underran Kahtanka, a near fatal advantage. Kahtanka gave ground; The Watcher's head twisted and heaved for the killing thrust beneath the chest. Then a tree bole at his rear steadied Kahtanka and a full-powered sweep of the head heaved the other up and flung him back. In this swift rally there was the element of surprise, and The Watcher hung at pause to collect his powers. When they came together again Kahtanka was carrying the aggression for the first time, his coordination returning in the heat of conflict.

Foot by foot the struggle worked up over a hillock and downslope toward the river. Their horns locked from time to time, then disengaged to rip and tear at neck and shoulder. At times both bulls were down on their knees, breath rasping, eye glaring into eye. Then up again to twist and prod and parry with swift-pivoting horns the side thrusts of the other. Flaps of skin and fur hung down from the heads and shoulders of each and in spots their heavy wool was red and sodden with blood.

Hours passed; the afternoon sun was yellowing but the battle still went on, the wrath-aroused powers of Kahtanka balancing now The Watcher's prime condition and dark determination. The last locking of horns had continued endlessly with no break on either side. A great circle of bulls and cows had formed around them by this time and the grunting and bellowing from the sidelines could be heard for miles. The stamina of The Watcher seemed never to flag, but in Kahtanka there was that which matched it in spite of all handicap, a proud and total inability to give in while life lasted—the heritage of the master breed.

Very slightly now, for a moment at a time, Kahtanka began to give ground, with a purpose. Each time The Watcher surged in with renewed fury to override, and Kahtanka, just avoiding the straight-on clash, slipped aside, bringing his sharp horn tips into play. Each of these times the inexorable pressure would slacken for a brief space in which Kahtanka subtly revived. To rally for one last effort was his purpose, else the other would slowly wear him down and win.

Sunset shadows had lengthened when Kahtanka's moment finally came. The abruptness with which he withdrew his horns pitched The Watcher forward, all asprawl. In that instant Kahtanka was around and under from the left side, the heart side, and with a mighty upthrust had hung the other on his horns. With a heave and a roar, Kahtanka pressed the advantage, boring in to rip and twist again and yet again, heaving the other's bulk aloft and finally toppling him like a statue from its base. Ruthlessly then Kahtanka tore in to the enemy's life-streams and when he had done a crashing salute sounded from the watching bulls, a blare of recognition and tribute to a new king.

CHAPTER ELEVEN

Sun Dance

STANDING ELK had a vision of a storm in which the clouds were white men's faces. As the clouds advanced upon the Sioux people, thunder crashed and lightning pierced the clouds, dissolving the faces into rain, which poured down upon the people. To the *shaman* this meant that more war was at hand. With Sitting Bull at the head of the nation he knew that there would be Sioux victories, but great losses also on both sides. To the Sioux all losses were vital. To the white man losses meant little, for their numbers in the east were beyond counting, as once the buffalo had been on the plains. In spite of any and all treaties the white men kept coming ever faster, by boat, by wagon train, in armed companies and now, more than ever before, by train.

The railroad had wrought an even greater evil. It had divided the great Continental Herd and to the south of the tracks the buffalo were dwindling like snow in the rain. Word had come in from Cheyenne and Comanche hunters that the southern herd was already nearly gone. Now, by Sitting Bull's orders, the northern herd was being watched over and actually herded by the Sioux in the hills of western Dakota and Montana. Some of the bison had moved still farther north and become, like the antelope, wild and swift, making new trails.

Great had been the trials for both buffalo and Indian. To Standing Elk by day and by night the air was burdened by the *pahaiyaane*, voices of the dead, and now those calling shadow bands were of man as well as animal. For the way of the buffalo was the way of the Sioux and their destinies were one. The *shaman* feared for his people. But not even to Horned Thunder did he voice his visions these days, for the Sioux were riding a wave of war and victory. Sitting Bull himself seemed blind to what surely must come. Nightly the drums sounded and the young men stamped out the hot beat of combat.

More than ever was Standing Elk thankful for Stabs-The-Bear, his foster son and co-worker. In him he clearly saw his own worthy successor in the medicine lodge. Between them they crushed the kernel of truth out of the silence and cast away the useless husk. In addition Stabs-The-Bear was a healer of troubles, a bringer-together among the people.

Sadly, from the standpoint of the *shaman*, Stabs-The-Bear was also a warrior. He would not be relegated to the ranks of the women and old men in this time of warfare. Lameness, he said, should not stop the warrior; Sitting Bull himself was lame. Stabs-The-Bear had become a masterful horseman and rifle shot and had taken many *coups* in the ever-increasing encounters with the white soldiers. For now the white men had sent an army against the Sioux under one called General "Long Hair" Custer. It was this one who had opened up the Sioux hunting grounds to white settlers, and built the "Thieves Road" into the Black Hills when gold was found there.

As for the *shaman's* own son, Hawk, he lived only for war. In the ten snows that had passed since Hawk had killed his first buffalo, the young brave had fought in twelve major engagements against the whites, some of them against the soldiers, some against the hide hunters. In these he had counted first *coups*. Hawk had *coups* also for rescuing wounded friends; once he had recovered the body of a chief under fire. Hawk had acquired many enemy horses, and had been hit three times by enemy bullets. Long ago Cetan the Swift had been shot from under him.

Once Hawk had captured a Crow warrior and his squaw in battle, but later spared them in honor of his brother Stabs-The-Bear, bravest of all the Crows. He was a member of several warrior societies and had three new names for his brave deeds, one of them bestowed by Horned Thunder himself: Man-Becoming-More. But he was still called Hawk and preferred to be known by his boyhood name.

Just now the *shaman* was thinking that Hawk might well have been named Man-Who-Is-Never-Satisfied, for today, preparatory to joining the united warriors of the Sioux under Sitting Bull, Hawk was beginning the ordeal of the Sun Dance. Few there were even among the Strong Hearts who would volunteer for such torture.

Early that morning the sacred tree, a cottonwood, had been cut down and stripped of its branches, and warriors were now setting it up in the center of camp. A cross-piece was fastened to the pole and to this were attached two small images, one of a man and one of a buffalo.

When the drums began to beat, Standing Elk left his tipi to watch with others of the elders. This was a variation of the Sun Dance ceremony, similar to that which Sitting Bull had recently undergone. But instead of resting on a buffalo robe to receive the cuts as the chief had done, Hawk stood upright while two warriors began cutting small pieces of skin and flesh from his arms and shoulders. These small wounds were Hawk's formal sacrifice to *Wah-kan-Tanka*, the Great One, and his prayer was for Sioux victory in coming battles. Without sound or the least flinching on the part of the sun dancer the cuttings continued, ten, twenty, thirty, forty cuts, while the blood trickled down between Hawk's curled fingers and dripped to the ground. Nor would forty cuts be enough. For as the *shaman* knew, Hawk's ordeal must equal that of Sitting Bull himself, who had offered up fifty pieces of skin and flesh.

When the cutting was over Hawk began the movements of the dance. His face lifted to the high June sun and he chanted with the rest.

Two warrior friends who had joined Hawk at the beginning of the dance dropped out as the shadows grew long. Hawk continued, turning slowly as the sun turned, facing always into its burning eye. Only after the sun had sunk below the horizon did he drop down on the mat of dried buffalo grass prepared for him, to lie without food or water through the night.

Next day, as the sun appeared over the eastern hills, Hawk was waiting to outgaze it. At intervals, spreading his arms wide, his cried out to *Wahkan-Tanka*. As before, his prayer was for victory for his people in the great battle all knew was coming soon. In the night he had dreamed of fast-firing enemy guns bursting like stars about his face. Then in his dream a real star had fallen out of the sky, shooting straight down upon him. His father would know the meaning of this dream, so would his brother Stabs-The-Bear. As for himself, he was not a dream-teller, but he vowed this dance would go on, without food or water, regardless of the torment of his swollen arms and burning eyes, until he collapsed.

The second day was a blazing one, very hot. Hawk's tongue was badly swollen and at times weakness bore him down, but he would not give in.

Once when the sun was sinking earthward and exhaustion and sleep almost overcame him, Hawk rubbed sweat-moistened tobacco in his eyes to stab himself awake.

By this time the whole camp was watching tensely, all sensing that Hawk was outdoing himself and that *Wahkan-Tanka* must surely answer. In the closest circle of watchers stood Stabs-The-Bear, pouring forth strength to his brother, trying to sustain his consciousness when it dimmed with pain. For hours also the *shaman* had been watching his son's dance. Toward sunset Standing Elk withdrew to the hills, for a great agony of premonition had been growing in him and he wished to pray alone.

In the early dark the *shaman* returned to his tipi and the small fire that burned there. Presently Stabs-The-Bear came in, glowing with pride.

"He sleeps again upon his mat, my father," he said.

"Did he drink and eat?" the *shaman* asked.

"He would touch nothing! He is not nearly finished! They are saying that this dance equals Sitting Bull's own. Always my brother Hawk has been a great warrior. Soon, very soon, he will be a great chief! Nothing ever stops that one!"

Standing Elk continued to gaze into the fire. His gray braids, wrapped in otter skin, lifted and fell with his breathing.

"Truly, Hawk will rise like the sun," he said at last. "So long as he may live," he added.

Stabs-The-Bear was transfixed by the thing not said, and for a moment bore the cold weight of portent. When he spoke, the young man did not ask for explanation. "You have had a vision, my father. Others have had visions also after watching my brother Hawk." He waited now for the *shaman* to speak again.

Standing Elk said, "It is to be feared that for this victory Hawk seeks for the people, the Great One will exact a price beyond that of the fifty pieces of skin and flesh."

Again Stabs-The-Bear waited, drawing for the explanation by not asking.

"Tonight in the hills," the *shaman* went on, "I howled like a wolf and a wolf howled back at me! Not once but twice. There will be death soon, much death; meat for the wolves. The great battle comes sooner than we think."

Stabs-The-Bear answered quietly, "We are ready, my father. We are strong. We are eager to meet the

Blue Coats. For have we not learned the kind of enemy we fight? Men who call it victory to ride into a Cheyenne village that has made peace and shoot down people of all ages! In this great battle that is coming, my father, our people will win!" Stabs-The-Bear's eyes flashed in the firelight.

The *shaman* inclined his head. "Yet though we win here and win there, the Blue Coats will keep pouring out of the east like a mighty flood. There is no end of them. But there is an end of us, because there is an end, already seen, of our buffalo herds! As always we and our totem are one. It is that we ourselves are as a small herd of buffalo surrounded by those hunters with the fast-shooting guns."

"Today, watching my brother dance," replied Stabs-The-Bear, "I could feel strength in my breast! And I know that many others felt the same. Perhaps, my father, there is some great plan in the mind of our chief whom we go to join on the Little Bighorn."

Standing Elk said solemnly, "We will pray for this. Pray also for Hawk, who goes too far in this dance, as in all things."

NOW IT WAS the third day of the Sun Dance. Still without water or food, with heavy, fevered arms and

eyes burned almost shut, Hawk faced the sun and
shuffled in the ritual motion, invoking victory. The
crowd about him scarcely moved. The sun mounted
higher and higher until Hawk was gazing straight
upward, head back upon his shoulders. In his weak-
ened state he often swayed, yet somehow kept his
balance. *Wahkan-Tanka* had heard him, all the
watchers knew now, yet still Hawk did not end his
dance-prayer.

The *shaman*, who prayed better alone, had withdrawn to the medicine lodge, but Stabs-The-Bear
was with his brother, standing ever closer as the sun
swung lower. Not until the gazer's eye was leveled
toward the west for the third time, did the over-
strained body falter and drop, though the will that
had driven it still knew no stopping. It was Stabs-
The-Bear who caught Hawk as he fell, and White
Antelope helped to carry the boy to the lodge of
Standing Elk.

Though the ordeal of the Sun Dance would have
killed many men, a single sleep and the good buffalo
broth that Willow Woman prepared, restored Hawk
so that further rest was irksome to the young warrior. As Hawk sat in the lodge opening, the *shaman*
was aware of the deep change that had come upon

his son. Hawk was quieter of spirit as well as of body, steadier of eye and sure of himself in a way that needed no proving. Something of the fire-eater had passed away. For the first time since he was a small boy, Standing Elk's spirit clasped that of his own blood son.

THE GREAT CAMP of the several Sioux tribes stretched for two miles along the bank of the Little Bighorn. Though the sun had only just reached its highest point of the year it was very dry and hot, and the sides of the tipis were rolled up to catch any stir of air. The men leaned back against the poles and drowsed, and the women were listless about their work today.

When the Oglala under Horned Thunder rode in and took their allotted place among the tribal circles, they had to drive their ponies nearly a mile to find forage, for the many animals of the big camp had already grazed off all the feeding close at hand.

All the tribes of the prairie Sioux were represented here: Hunkpapa, Blackfeet, Brule, Minniconjou, Sans Arc, Two Kettle and Oglala. There were also many friendly Cheyenne and Arapahoe visitors from the west, and their greatest chiefs. Sitting Bull had called them here for he knew that the recent Sioux victory in the valley of the Rosebud was only a beginning.

The Oglala under Crazy Horse were wild with that recent victory, in which they had routed the troops under General "Three Star" Crook, and they were eager for more. Scouts had brought in word that Three Star was still marching his men away from the region. But other word had come in that "Long Hair" Custer himself was coming and was now not far away.

When Horned Thunder's band saw Chief Sitting Bull coming toward their circle, he and White Antelope, Standing Elk, and several of the Strong Hearts, Hawk among them, moved forward to meet him. Today the buckskin shirt the chief wore was embroidered with green porcupine quills and he wore a single eagle feather at the back of his head. He carried a flywhisk made of a buffalo tail bound to a stick. Not tall, heavily built, and broad of face, with a limp from an old wound, Sitting Bull nevertheless had the dignity, the sure and unhurried presence of the great chief that he was.

Without preliminary he began talking, not as one who opens a subject, but as one who speaks from the very heat of it, as indeed was the case. For since the rising of the sun he had been moving from circle to circle, holding council with chiefs and warriors.

"Friends," he said, "you all know why we are here together and what we await. The Blue Coats under Long Hair himself are coming this way. They bring war and we will meet them with war. It is said that they come seeking the Hunkpapa and me. They will find the whole Sioux Nation waiting for them. You all know what happened in the valley of the Rosebud. It must happen again here on the Bighorn, only now we must kill all, before they slaughter us as they have slaughtered our herds. Already to the south the buffalo are gone. Soon it will be the same here in the north unless we kill the killers. So long as there are any buffalo or Sioux left we will fight! There are buffalo left because our braves have herded and protected them through this bad time. And there are Sioux left, I see."

This was said with a glint of eye and a wide gesture that swept the teeming encampment. "I see, too, that there is one here with the scars of the Sun Dance scarcely dry upon him." The piercing yet kindly eyes of the chief had singled out Hawk and the broad mouth twitched faintly in his special smile. "Such a one needs no word from me except a brother's greeting."

Not long ago such recognition from the chief would have overwhelmed Hawk, but in the new sureness that had come to him since the Sun Dance he took it with a stoic calm.

"Friends," Sitting Bull continued, "there will be great fighting here on the Bighorn! And it must be cold fighting like the Blue Coats' own war. Not the way of the Sioux brave who dashes in to count *coup* and dashes out again, but a charging in all together to kill and kill and kill that our people may survive!"

CHAPTER TWELVE

The Little Bighorn

NEXT MORNING, soon after the horses had been taken to water, a cry went up from the river bank. A boy came running in with the report that his companion had been shot by soldiers. The boy pointed south, up-river, and there above the hills dust was rising, telling it to every circle of the great combined village.

Now in each band war chiefs already mounted were calling out orders to the young men and instructing the elders to take charge of the women and children. Though all seemed utter confusion, with warriors running for their horses, women collecting their frightened children, and dogs scuttling about in everyone's way, actually the preparations to meet the attack were swift and thorough.

Hawk, who had been decorating his horse with the colors of war, mounted swiftly and sped to the *shaman's* lodge for his Winchester and cartridge belt, also his shield, his war club and knife for hand-to-hand fighting. The tipi was already empty. Standing Elk was busy directing the flight of the women north to safer ground and Willow Woman was helping with the small ones who had to be carried. Some of the women were trying to cross the stream in the way of the warriors and the *shaman* was calling them back.

Hawk lifted a hand to his father as he rode out to join the fighting men. From every camp warriors were riding forth. Now the blue coats of soldiers and their horses' heads were visible above a rise to the south. Partly to cover the retreat of the women and children, many of the braves plunged across the stream with loud war cries. Hawk saw Chief Sitting Bull on his black war horse coming along the stream bank.

"Remember we fight to kill!" he was calling out to group after group of braves. "Charge all together! Keep charging! Kill all!"

As Hawk joined White Antelope's band and crossed the stream, the soldiers on the slope above opened fire. There was only a thin line of the Blue Coats and opposing them hundreds of Sioux massing for a charge. Seeing this the soldiers retreated to the timber on the bluff, dismounted, and reformed their line.

"*Hopo! Hopo!* Spread out and surround them!" called White Antelope.

The soldiers were firing in earnest now as the Oglala, together with many Hunkpapa and some Cheyennes, charged them from both north and west. The ends of the enemy line broke and many soldiers were shot or brought down with bow and arrow. The soldiers' central position held for a time, then they began dropping back farther into the timber, though keeping up a steady fire. Soon their line was behind a steep cutbank and the advancing Sioux were all about them. Hawk heard White Antelope crying out that these could not be Long Hair's troops because Long Hair himself was not among them.

Hawk saw the Blue Coats' chief running this way and that, shouting. He looked afraid and so he might be, for the Sioux far outnumbered his soldiers. But with white men you never knew; it might be some trick. More of the Long Knives might be coming to reinforce him.

Now White Antelope rallied the Oglala fighters and a wave of them, with some of the Hunkpapa, swept forward, once more putting the Long Knives on either flank of the company to flight. But again the soldiers in the center held. Galloping in among the fleeing troops, the Sioux killed with rifles, arrows and war clubs. In Hawk's ears were the words of Sitting Bull: *Kill! Kill!*

In a rush of power he overtook a mounted soldier, jerked him from the saddle, and killed him with a single blow of his war club as a hunter kills a rabbit with a swift blow behind the ears. The blood of the Long Knife ran warm on his hand and he dropped the body. Hawk was dismounted momentarily to retrieve the soldier's rifle, and lashed the flank of the riderless horse to drive it out of the path of the fighting. Before he could remount, a soldier ahead swung about and took aim at him. A sudden movement was his only chance and Hawk leapt to the side, away from his horse instead of into the saddle, as the enemy would expect. The bullet whined in the air he had just quitted. Before the Long Knife confronting him could shoot again, Hawk killed him with the rifle of the first dead soldier.

More than thirty Blue Coats now lay dead upon the slope, but no one bothered to count *coup*. As Hawk swung back with the others, a volley from the troops that had held their ground brought down five of the braves. The Sioux circled again, toward the stream, pouring bullets and arrows into the final cluster of soldiers. These were routed from among the trees, the last four men leading the horses. Hawk and two other braves were about to overhaul these when a shout from Chief Sitting Bull himself came from the river bank.

"Let them go! Let them live to tell the truth about this battle! They started this fight! We did not!"

Obeying, Hawk and the other braves turned back and began tending their wounded. Stabs-The-Bear was there, just lifting young Swift Otter across his horse. Hawk helped him, then together they lifted another wounded brave of the Hunkpapa onto Hawk's horse. Riding close together they returned to the nearly empty camp circle. Their father was in the medicine lodge tending to some of the wounded that had been brought there. Standing Elk's eyes lit with gratitude at sight of his sons alive and unhurt, but from his manner they knew that he had bad news from his communings.

"More of the enemy are coming," he told them. "Very many of them are coming now."

"That is the trick then," Hawk said. "They were too few, the others."

Even now, as Hawk and Stabs-The-Bear came out of the medicine lodge, the general alarm was heard:

"*Hoye, hoye!* More Blue Coats are coming!"

Soon another group of soldiers could be seen on the bluffs across the stream, very many this time. Hawk and his brother mounted their horses again and joined the other warriors. As they moved down to the stream bank to cross once more, line after line of soldiers came into view, raising clouds of dust in the hot summer air. There was the sound of bugles and colored streamers flapped above the heads of the mounted men. Now some of the Blue Coats moved down toward the river. Four braves, all of them Cheyennes, plunged their horses across the stream to confront them. The line of soldiers stopped and shooting began. Puffs of powder smoke rolled along the hillside until the enemy could scarcely be seen.

It was into this murk of dust and smoke that the brothers rode with many of their friends, others massing behind them. They plunged across the stream and up the slope in full cry. In the density now it was as if each man fought alone; Hawk could scarcely discern the enemy as he emptied his rifle.

Half way up the ridge the haze cleared somewhat. Many of the enemy and some Sioux lay dead on the hillside. Others of the Blue Coats were fleeing up the bank, all but a small band of mounted men, on whom the warriors converged. Soon these turned and fled with scores of Sioux and Cheyenne in close pursuit, shooting them out of their saddles or pulling them to the ground and killing them with tomahawks. It had turned into a rout. The Sioux were grimly carrying out the orders of their chief to kill all.

Young South Bear's leg brushed Hawk's in passing and he shouted, "It is like running buffalo!"

"But I have not seen Long Hair!" Hawk called back. "These cannot be his men!"

Some of the braves were turning back now to round up the enemy horses and collect whatever guns and ammunition were to be found. Hawk was among those who pressed on to the top of the ridge.

Here the remaining soldiers had dismounted quickly, bunched together, and were pouring a concerted rifle fire down the slope. The Sioux advance was checked. Scattering now, and most of them on foot, the warriors snatched such weapons and ammunition as they could from the fallen troopers and deployed through brush for a fresh attack.

Hawk himself had taken an army pistol, two rifles, both of them better and newer than the one Stabs-The-Bear had given him, and as much ammunition as he could carry. Finding himself alone again, he worked his way up a narrow gully to the left of the enemy, presently joining a party of Hunkpapa fighting men, all armed with enemy guns. White Bull, Sitting Bull's nephew, was leading these.

Now every ravine and gully was filled with Sioux and Cheyenne warriors creeping toward the top of the ridge where the soldiers had made their stand. The firing upon the enemy began from three sides, increasing steadily as more warriors came up. The fire from the troops never slackened, but they were greatly outnumbered and the Sioux had cover of a sort in the brush-grown approaches, while the soldiers stood exposed. Their numbers diminished swiftly and visibly.

It was White Bull who gave the order for hand-to-hand fighting with the remaining soldiers. Hawk was in the first line of braves that rushed the enemy. A white soldier fired almost in his face as he sprang in with a loud war cry. Hawk felt the very wind of the bullet's passing but was unhurt. The soldier aimed again but the hammer clicked on an empty cartridge so he hurled the gun at Hawk. Dodging, Hawk closed with the man. They rolled over twice in the dust, then Hawk freed his arm and his knife sank deep.

Another Blue Coat sprang in upon him from the side, one of the enemy chiefs, for he wore three colored stripes on his blue sleeve. This man was very strong and young, with a black beard covering his chin and running up his white cheek. Hawk whirled to grip him, but two big hands closed around his neck and pressed in his windpipe. They went down, the soldier's grip tightening, his knees bludgeoning Hawk's body, for this white man fought with every inch of him.

The bright sun was dimming in Hawk's eyes and he was dying a little death before the strength came to him to raise one leg for the planting of a foot and one arm, elbow down, to throw his punisher off. This was a Sioux wrestling trick and the man went over on his back. But before Hawk could pin him down he had snatched his pistol and fired. The bullet was like a scald across Hawk's bare ribs, but just before the second shot was fired Hawk was in, kicking the weapon from the other's hand and falling upon him with his knife.

Now there were but some twenty soldiers left standing, Sioux fighters ringing them round. Blood was running down Hawk's chest and his side was numb, but he was still able to fight. He heard a call for help off to the side and saw White Bull rolling on the ground in the grip of a tall soldier with short light hair. The soldier had White Bull's braids in his two hands and had drawn his head down and was biting his face. Help was needed there, but Hawk could not shoot for fear of hitting White Bull. And to reach White Bull's side he had to thread the crossfire of the enemy and his own people.

Hawk started on all fours, carrying a rifle in his right hand. The distance was some forty yards and he had covered half of it when a carbine bullet from the weapon of a downed soldier struck him like an ax-blow, spinning him onto his back. Hawk lay there looking at the man who had fired the shot and saw the smoking rifle drop from his hands as a Sioux bullet killed him.

Up the slope Hawk heard White Bull's call again. He tried to crawl, but blinding pain flattened him to earth. Dimly he saw that Bear Lice and another Hunkpapa man had run to aid White Bull. The fighters were whirling over and over now. Then Hawk heard four shots of a pistol and though the sun was darkening for his eyes he was able to see that the three Hunkpapa were standing above the body of the white man.

THERE WAS a rocking and a swaying and both were great pain. When Hawk's eyes opened he was slumped forward over the neck of a horse. Stabs-The-Bear was holding him for he heard the voice of his brother behind him. The battle was not yet entirely over, for bullets whined round them. Hawk knew he was bleeding badly and that blackness was trying to take him again. In spite of himself a groan was wrenched from him and he felt Stabs-The-Bear's hand close strongly on his shoulder.

"We will soon be in camp. You made a good fight, my brother. You collected many feathers."

The horse stumbled on a loose stone and Hawk groaned again. Stabs-The-Bear's chest was covered with Hawk's blood. He uttered some brave grunts to help his brother. Hawk echoed them and the blackness drew back for a little space before it closed over him.

LATER THAT DAY smoke clouds rolled all along the banks of the Bighorn where the Sioux had set the prairie grass ablaze in token of victory. It was a great victory indeed, for of the second and larger party of Blue Coats to attack them, not a soldier had been left alive. But in the combined Sioux village all was quiet that night, for many brave warriors had died.

In the dawn of the next morning the big camp began to break up. From the opening of the medicine lodge Standing Elk watched band after band of his friends hurriedly departing. None knew better than the *shaman* the reason for their haste. More soldiers would be coming, a blue flood of them. The Sioux might fight to the end but there would never be an end of the Long Knives. They were beyond counting. Sitting Bull, too, knew this well.

"We cannot stay here," he had said after the battle. "And there are but two ways to go now, to the Land of the Grandmother, or the Land of the Spaniards. For me, I choose the Land of the Grandmother."

But the camp of the Oglala would be going nowhere for a while, for all his friends had agreed to remain with Hawk through his bad time. Throughout the night just past Standing Elk and Stabs-The-Bear had worked over the wounded one. In between his sleeps of pain and weakness Hawk's mind was clear. He would ask for details of the battle and what Sitting Bull had said. Answering, the *shaman* would rejoice in the strength of his son's spirit, though his communings through the long night had shown no hope. True, wounds as grave as Hawk's had been healed before with fungus to stop the bleeding, and herbs to aid the strength, and prayers to the Great One to sustain life. But Standing Elk's heart knew. A time had ended with the battle on the Little Bighorn. The freedom and power of the Sioux had passed with this great victory, and Hawk, who was of that freedom and that power, was passing with them.

As he watched from the lodge opening, the *shaman* saw a cluster of excited elders gathering before a tipi not far away. He joined them to hear the news. A Hunkpapa man had just ridden in from Fort Abraham Lincoln. This man knew General Custer by sight and it was Long Hair himself he had just seen among the dead up on the ridge. The general had had his hair cut before this battle so that he would not be recognized and none of the Sioux had known him. In fact none had known until now that it was Long Hair's army that their warriors had killed to the last man.

This news only deepened Standing Elk's growing sense of finality as he hastened back to his son's side. Hawk was awake again and Stabs-The-Bear was kneeling beside him holding a horn spoon full of broth which Willow Woman had made. Hawk turned his face away from the food, but there was a smile for his father as he came close.

"What is the news now, my father?" he asked.

The *shaman* told him, adding, "They are saying it was White Bull of the Hunkpapa who killed Long Hair Custer."

"Then I saw him die!" Hawk said. "*Ho Hechetu!* That was a fight! I was trying to get to White Bull when that bullet came. So he is dead now, our worst enemy! Truly we have won a great victory, and there will be many more, with Sitting Bull to lead us. I will rejoin him as soon as I can ride!"

The *shaman* raised a hand to quiet his warlike son, for such excitement as burned in him was taking the small balance of his strength. Hawk's head fell back.

"He sleeps again, my father!" said Stabs-The-Bear.

But Standing Elk's heart knew better as he looked down at the still form by the fire.

CHAPTER THIRTEEN

Medicine Bull

THE NEW TRAILS Kahtanka had chosen for the herd were old trails now, and habit had made them good. But there came the spring when a new and strange thing occurred on their journey north. They had wintered west of the Bad Lands and had moved north to the Little Missouri when the thaws came. There a great cordon of mounted men with feathers in their hair confronted them, blocking their natural course north to the upper reaches of the Yellowstone where April always drew them. There were wild cries and the roar of many guns, yet no death in the herd. The ranks were merely forced back upon themselves.

Kahtanka waited until the following day and tried again to lead his herd northward. Again dark riders poured down upon them from the surrounding hills, even more of them this time, yelling and shooting into the air until the ranks surged in upon themselves in terror. Not an animal had been killed, but a restless frustration possessed the mass. Kahtanka went to a lookout knoll to feel this strange thing out.

This was the familiar pattern, the leader withdrawing to await the call. The herd's tension grounded and the animals fed. At the right time the signal would come to move. Lesser bulls were posted at strategic points to relay the master's slightest order. The rest of the herd dispersed along the river bank below to drink and bathe and wallow. By late afternoon all knew that only sudden attack would move them that day. They rested, their trust in their leader complete.

With the morning, Kahtanka's faith, too, had returned. They would move northward now as they always had done; it was time, and what had happened yesterday was forgotten. His single signal passed from bull to bull and to the leading cows throughout the ranks, and automatically all were in motion. It was not the travel lope of autumn, but the pace was as fast as the many heavy cows would permit.

At the mouth of the valley they must follow, they were met by a line of riders and it all began again. At first it was like an attack. For attack they were prepared, if afterwards they could move on. But there were no death-bawls, no blood smell, only the fearsome yells and the great explosions of sound, and once more the herd resistlessly folded back upon itself.

All that day the Indian riders stayed in sight, showing at times on the hilltops or circling the far edges of the herd, and that night there were campfires and the smell of smoke. For days thereafter all actual passage was blocked. To the north were the Bighorn mountains, to the south lay their own tabu, the railroad. In this region of some hundred square miles, other buffalo which the Sioux had rounded up before Kahtanka's band were also being herded. When white hunters came into this area, which was still Sioux territory, they were attacked and driven out as if they had brought war to the Sioux themselves.

In the bison spirit migration was as ingrained as

breeding or eating. Kahtanka waited, carrying on his
daily affairs of feeding, ruminating, wallowing, and
watching from his lookout, but always he was keyed
to a possible break-through of the barrier to the
north. The sense of *The Wall* grew and grew, until it
never left him, even in sleep. Not only had he lost
the immemorial freedom of the plains and trails, but
now his very dreams were invaded and fenced about
by the enemy. This final restriction Kahtanka could
not endure.

It was midday, the drowsing time, but Kahtanka
was already in motion, his angry bellow whipping
five younger bulls to their feet, two of them mud-
caked from the wallows, and three old leading cows.
Up the hill toward the smoke of the nearest campfires he pounded with the eight at his back, blasting
out challenges, though as yet unaware of the reason.

The Sioux herders, chewing pemmican by their
small fire, were taken by surprise. They leapt up,
dodging aside like harried rabbits, but one of them
was caught and tossed high in the air. Two tethered
horses were heaved aloft on black horns and trampled to death. The buffalo swept on, and the Sioux,
when they had collected themselves and their remaining horses, gave chase. Even then there was no

shooting, for all this herding of bison was in accordance with an edict of Chief Sitting Bull's to round up and protect the last of the great north herd.

Not before late afternoon were the nine rebels circled by a far-flung cordon of Indians. Kahtanka permitted this; for the moment of his fury was spent. Night was coming on and already he was lonely for Beaverskin and his family.

Now calving time of the first year of captivity was at hand and migration was quite naturally curtailed. The grazing was good, there was ample water, and the peace and somnolence of another summertime was beginning. The luring pictures of the northern feeding grounds grew dim, but not the mutiny in Kahtanka's blood. With the life design of the herd broken, his very power of leadership was thrust back upon itself, and out of inaction new instincts arose. When the rhythm of the land was one with the pulse of his own heart and blood, that place was sanctuary. Here, though there was no killing and there was ample water and feeding, the land warned continually of danger and death to come. Clearer and clearer the warning sounded, but it was for him alone, for the herd in general was dulled by this false peace.

There were periods when Kahtanka waited and

watched in apparent somnolence, but never for a moment did he forget that escape was the goal. Abruptly out of his stillness he would erupt into violent action: charge a particular section of the lazing herd and deliberately haze the mass into cross-country flight. A few days later it would be another wing of the herd he harried awake. He was like a drill sergeant conditioning troops, for rigor and strife had always been the bisons' wild true life.

On occasion it was not his own ranks that he harassed, but the enemy itself, the mounted herders. Inevitably came the day when he overtook another rider, South Bear, as it happened, and destroyed both the man and his horse. That same day he whipped the herd into a stampede which finally took every Sioux rider within a radius of fifty miles to circumvent.

That night in the Oglala camp there was a council fire and much talk. Horned Thunder heard the many complaints from the chief of the herders, Otter Tail. The death of South Bear was told and retold in details and the former warrior eulogized. Then the stampede that had followed was recounted by a number of riders who helped to stop it. All of this as well as the death of young Wind Singer and the horses that were also killed that day was said to be the work of a single black bull. Otter Tail advised the immediate destruction of this renegade.

"It may be," said Horned Thunder. "But how is one certain that it is the same bull?"

"A master bull and black," said Otter Tail, "and truly the same one because of his great size and the white mark on his forehead which all have seen."

"Then this talk of destroying is a real word," said Horned Thunder seriously. "But master bulls are few and the best are needed to renew the herd. We must think long and well."

"But nothing is safe with that one in the herd!" Otter Tail replied. "That one is always thinking, like a bear. He will attack again and who may say what will happen?"

"A black bull with a white mark on the forehead, you say?" The voice came from the far edge of the firelight. It was Standing Elk, rousing from a doze. The *shaman* had not been well since the death of his son Hawk, and though he attended all councils he often dropped off during the lengthy formalities. Tonight, though the air was warm, he was wrapped to the nose in his blanket.

The *shaman* was answered by Horned Thunder.

"It is a black master bull of the herd that has caused much trouble, Grandfather. Yes, a white mark on the forehead that all have seen."

"What troubles are these?" Standing Elk asked.

Patiently and in detail, while all waited, Horned Thunder recounted the story. The *shaman* was silent in thought for a time, then began his questions, though each question was like an answer to what had gone before.

"This bull, you say, does not submit in peace to being herded? Since the old ways are denied him, this bull at times attacks what blocks the way of his people—even though that be armed men and fires? Also, you say, he disciplines his followers to keep them ready and fit for the trail? And this one, this medicine bull, has a white mark like a star on his forehead?"

"So it is, my uncle," said Otter Tail.

The *shaman* let his thoughts sink back through the years. Could this be the very black bull with the starred brow whose birth he had witnessed so many springs ago, and met a second time on the Yellowstone, whose way he had strengthened all through the years with prayer and strong medicine? Truly it must be!

"Let our people take hope from this thing!" Standing Elk said, suddenly strong of voice. "Has so much evil come upon us then—and so much death—that the buffalo is not still the Sioux totem? Here is one whose spirit will not be broken! He fights on for his people as our own leader, Sitting Bull, is doing."

His words struck home to his listeners. This was the year following the battle on the Little Bighorn, now called "The Custer Massacre" by the whites, and all the plains Indians, the Sioux in particular, were blamed and hated and harried for it. Many of the tribes had already gone into the agencies, but Sitting Bull still had a thousand warriors on Grand River, and Crazy Horse and his Oglala were with him. There were also other large bands of Sioux close by, but all were kept in continuous movement and frequent flight by the Blue Coats. It had become more than ever necessary for the Sioux to preserve such buffalo as they could in the heart of their own territory.

Standing Elk continued: "What did Sitting Bull say when Three Stars Crook sent word to surrender or he would kill all? 'I will be the last man to lay down my gun!' That was the answer Sitting Bull sent back! And this answer heartened our people! Even though many of our tribes have buried the hatchet and gone in to the white man's agencies, there is one great one who remains fearless and free, like this bull you would now kill!"

Hau's and grunts of approval went around the firelit circle. Presently Horned Thunder addressed the council.

"It is now clear," he told them, "that this medicine bull who thinks like a bear is not to be killed. It is for the herders also to think like bears."

TO IMPROVE the herd and build it up, the tribe killed only the scrubbiest animals for their immediate needs. But as is true of all captive things, breeding in the herd was curtailed and spiritless, with less rivalry and less combat than ever before, as if the bison spirit was experiencing a mood of finality in which all such excitements were bootless.

The southern herd was long since extinct. The Wyoming and Canada herds were almost gone. To the south, east, and west, white hunters had reaped great harvests of hides and meat. When it became generally known that the Sioux had rounded up and were literally riding herd on practically all of the bison left in the land, white men from far-flung forts and settlements rode forth to try for a last tribute. Many of these had never seen a buffalo herd and they formed exuberant parties to savor this greatest of all frontier sports which would soon be gone forever. And for the most adventurous, the guardianship of the Indians but added to the zest of the hunt, particularly as all Sioux were hated now and classed as outlaws.

It was early in the second year of Kahtanka's captivity that a band of settlers from Fort Laramie forced their way through the thin line of Indian herders. Before the Sioux could gather in force some thirty animals had been killed. Then, outnumbered more than ten to one, the Laramie party retreated down the valley, using an old trick of the Sioux themselves to make good their escape. The wind was in their favor and they left the prairie grass blazing behind them, a fire which swept down in a wall upon the Sioux fighters, effectively putting them to flight and the buffalo as well.

Kahtanka and his section of the herd fled before the sea of flame in a rout which nothing could have stopped, and it was the following day before the flight really came to an end. By this time the band was far beyond Sioux territory. Kahtanka was now

pressing them by new trailless ways, south and east
whence the seasonal call came. In the river valley
into which they turned there was no definite goal, no
pressure of time, yet they were moving at a fast pace,
the old travel lope of fall and freedom. Kahtanka had
no need to press them now. The rhythm of the lope
was the natural release to long restraint and in it the
herd spirit was healed and unified.

Even deeper fulfillment came to them one day
when a small band of cows and young came out of a
side valley and eagerly joined them for company and
protection, quite as it had been in the old days. Later
that same afternoon they approached what might
have been a dark outcrop of stone in the middle of
the dun-colored plain. Nearer at hand it proved to
be a lone buffalo bull of great size, his wool bleached
with age, an old outcast evidently too tough to die
or be killed. The travelers surged around him, blasting and muttering in friendly fashion so that he was
surrounded, enfolded once more by his kind. Time
was, not too long before, when this grandfather had
dreamed of being one of a herd again and had longed
for little else. Now, crusty and indurated by solitude,
he was beyond response. The herd flowed round and
past him. Toward the end, in the last of the ranks,

the old one moved forward a few hundred feet as if drawn by a tenuous cord. But the cord snapped and he came to rest again, becoming once more a dark and moveless outcrop on the lonely plain.

Now the dangers of passage began to beset them once more. Well aware of their dwindled numbers, coyotes and lobo wolves gathered in packs and harried the herd even by day. Wherever they were sighted by humans, hunters rode out to take tribute, so that Kahtanka came to avoid every patch of timber or gap in the hills where an ambush might be waiting. Such hunters as did catch up with them had a run for their trophies, for this was a fast-moving, well-conditioned band—Kahtanka's own. Even so there was not a day but all the herd master's craft was needed.

They had reached the confluence of the Big and the Little Missouri. To the south, along the smaller stream, was a country of coulee-cut brush-land, a region where all trails ended where they began. Here the growth was often higher than a buffalo's shoulder and a sizable band could spread out and be lost to sight within a mile. For two days and nights the fugitives wound their way through ravine and thicket while Kahtanka felt out the pulse of the

place. There were waterholes along some of the cou-
lees. The twisting paths through the brush were
game trails made by their old neighbors of the plains,
the pronghorn antelope, and by wild cattle and mus-
tangs that roamed the region. Of man there was no
trace to be sensed. And soon it began to be evi-
dent that their weather-vanes, the cowbirds, also ap-
proved of this place. The sounds they now made
were quite other than the discontented raspings that
had gone on during the long-enforced stay in Sioux
territory.

Here, though the feeding was patchy and at times
sparse, the rhythm of the land was one with Kahtanka's own pulse and blood. This was sanctuary.

It was the refuge of the historic Last Thousand.

CHAPTER FOURTEEN

Wahkan-Tanka!

IN THIS NEW life in which there was no fighting and scarcely any uncertainty, Standing Elk was wont to think that there was little need of a *shaman*. Yet even here at the agency those of his people who wished for a dream-teller and prophet still came to his tipi and received counsel, the best that he could give under these new and strange conditions. For all life was changed here, and must change much more. The inside of the great log stockade was like a town, with streets and a store where rations were dealt out, and there was a church were the Indians were supposed to forget *Wahkan-Tanka* and all the sacred things of the past.

At this time there were still some die-hard remnants of the Sioux tribes at large, but most of the Oglala had accepted the inevitable and surrendered. Sitting Bull and his band had gone to Canada, as he had said he would.

A few concessions had been made by the whites. Those of the people who wished to live in tipis were allowed to do so, out behind the government barracks which housed most of the Indians. All the elders had kept their tipis, and Standing Elk's lodge stood beside the yellow-painted one of Chief Horned Thunder, as in the old days. But from the beginning the ancient tribal chants and dances were banned. These ceremonies were called "devil worship" by the white preacher. Nor could they wear any of the finery they once had, or use the old designs and symbols, for these things recalled the proud fierce ways of the past. But hardest for all of them in this new life was the staying in one place, which was as unnatural to Sioux nature as captivity was to the buffalo. From time beyond memory the plains Indians had moved with the herds according to the seasons.

Standing Elk had preserved his medicine bundle, filled with the sacred articles, and with these he could still show the way at times or assist in a cure. But he lacked many of the old herbs and more and more the sick were the special province of Stabs-The-Bear, who was a full-fledged *shaman* now. Always learning, that one, and learning still, even from the white medicine doctor here at the fort.

Soon after the Oglala under Horned Thunder had been forced into the agency, Willow Woman was taken ill. Privation and the tension of a driven and harried people, plus fear for Standing Elk's life, had brought her low with a strange illness so that she lay upon her blankets believing she would die. Wood Mouse was not there to help, for she had been married to a Hunkpapa brave before they entered the agency, but Standing Elk wrought by day and by night with Willow Woman, as did Stabs-The-Bear. To little effect, however, for her pain and her fears persisted.

"You are in danger of your life here," she would say to the *shaman,* rolling her head where the pain demon was greatest. "We cannot trust the word of this agency chief any more than the word of the Long Knives who killed all our buffalo and stole all our land! At any time they may decide to kill you."

This fear, Standing Elk knew, was because he had been a man of influence in the tribe and all such were suspect to the whites, their names known even before they entered the agencies. A number of chiefs and leaders had been "eliminated" immediately upon surrendering. Crazy Horse of the Oglala was one of these. He had surrendered in good faith at Red Cloud Agency, but was stabbed in the back by Indian police and died a few hours later. There was the story of Dull Knife of the Cheyennes, who surrendered with his people at Fort Robinson. Because one of the braves was missing one night, the entire band was locked up and starved for eight days and then shot. There was also the death of Spotted Tail, who had been a friend of both Sitting Bull and Crazy Horse. And Chief Joseph of the Nez Perce was dead at the white man's hands. All these deaths were called "accidents" by the whites, but the Sioux knew better.

Standing Elk tried to quiet Willow Woman: "The ones the white men have killed were chiefs and fighting men. I am a *shaman*."

"But you have had a voice in war," she argued shrewdly. "You have counseled the chiefs and warriors. All this is known."

"The whites claim they killed Crazy Horse and Spotted Tail because they were planning secret at-

tacks," Standing Elk said, although he did not believe it any more than did Willow Woman.

"If they have no reason to kill our great ones they
make a reason!" she replied. "It is that they are a-
fraid our chiefs will bring the tribes together and de-
feat the Long Knives again, as in the past."

To Stabs-The-Bear the *shaman* said: "This demon
of pain which Willow Woman suffers mocks all that
I know. If only I had the old herbs."

"I know the very ones," said Stabs-The-Bear understandingly. "In three suns I could ride to the
mountains and bring them back. But they will not
let anyone go for so long. One might bring the white
medicine man to my father's lodge," Stabs-The-Bear
added. "Many of the people were sick when they
came here and it is said that he has cured them."

The *shaman* was willing to try this, but at the very
thought of a white doctor in their tipi Willow Woman's pain became much worse. Watching her suffering, Stabs-The-Bear decided what he must do.

He could speak no English, but he had a Sans Arc
friend, Two Feathers, who agreed to translate for
him. And so, standing before the white doctor, Stabs-
The-Bear told all about the demon of pain his foster
mother suffered and Two Feathers told it all over

again to the white medicine man. The doctor smiled and nodded as if he already knew this demon, then reached to a shelf and brought down a bottle filled with strange white tablets and another bottle containing powder. To Two Feathers he gave directions: three times each sun for the pills and once at owl light for the powder, for Stabs-The-Bear's mother.

Very soon Willow Woman was feeling better, so that she rose from her blankets and set about cooking a meal for her husband and her foster son. Soon after this she was to be seen visiting with other squaws in the tipis close by.

The cure of his mother convinced Stabs-The-Bear of the healing power of the white man's medicine. He saw other cures with his own eyes, so when illness came upon friends he counseled trust in the craft of the white medicine man and even helped the doctor at his work. Meanwhile Stabs-The-Bear was learning to speak English and was becoming useful in many ways, not only to the doctor whom he assisted, but to the commandant of the fort.

When there were misunderstandings, when the gulf between red man and white seemed most impassable, it was Stabs-The-Bear who was sent to mediate. Whether it was a question of a trouble-making firebrand among the young, or a malcontent among the old, Stabs-The-Bear was the one to reach the heart of the matter and counsel away wrath. For the young *shaman* had learned that it was not only in silence, as his foster father had taught him, that the kernel of truth was pressed forth, but also by the grinding of two points of view.

Standing Elk was proud of his foster son, so quick in the mind, so helpful to his people. Stabs-The-Bear was young and this, the old *shaman* knew, made it easier for his foster son to understand new ways. Standing Elk hoped it was all for the best, but with no herd spirit to commune with, how could one be sure? Often the *shaman* felt that he had outlived his time, for he missed his religion overmuch. In this place ruled by the white man *Wahkan-Tanka*, the Great One, seemed withdrawn, like the Sioux totem itself. There had been few enough buffalo left when the Oglala came in to the agency, for even those the Sioux had guarded had dwindled to almost nothing. Since then the white killings had undoubtedly accounted for the rest.

Standing Elk lived now with the fear that there were no buffalo left at all. His apprehensive mind made black pictures. Sometimes he imagined the last small herd surrounded by white hunters and slaughtered to the last animal. Or he would see them cut down one by one by bears and lobo wolves, or winter-killed in the northern hills. The *shaman* brooded overmuch.

EVEN IN THE wild brush country of the Little Missouri Kahtanka's herd was discovered. In time hunters found them out, but these were comparatively few and in this place no mounted drive was possible. For the most part those who found them were still-hunters operating singly or in pairs. Even though the killings were few compared to the old days, they were quite as drastic for the diminished herd. In time the king bull himself, so clever in guarding his band, became the main object of most of these hunts. Even the occasional Indian who came that way sought the robe of the star-faced bull as a very special medicine. The fact that he was the last of his kind made him the rarest of trophies. Kahtanka carried numerous bullets and broken-off arrowheads in his great body, and upon his hide were the scars of many wounds, but his sagacity and his powers of endurance continued to frustrate the best-laid plans of his stalkers.

During the second year in the brush-land Beaver-skin had fallen to a still-hunter's rifle. Since calf-hood she had been Kahtanka's nearest companion, and the sharpest of his craft had been developed in her protection. When his brooding grief and loneli-ness had finally passed, this care and wisdom was de-voted wholly to his following, plus all the super wile he had learned since the day he first defied herd law and found a new resourcefulness. Kahtanka had be-come the greatest leader of his kind, not because he was king of vast numbers like the master bulls of the old Continental Herd, but because he brought his species through the terrible time of change.

Even so his band had dwindled to less than two hundred. It was reports of this remnant of the Last Thousand that awakened Government tardily to the near-extinction of the bison kind, and led to preser-vation measures. In the Yellowstone and in the west-ern Dakotas, as well as in Canada, small bands still existed, and to protect them laws were quickly en-acted prohibiting buffalo hunting. Groups of Gov-ernment men soon began rounding up all remaining bison and driving them into special preserves, fol-lowing out the plan of protection which the Sioux had had to abandon.

One of these bands of Government men appeared in the brush-land one day. The sight of Kahtanka fired them with an added zeal, and one of their number was dispatched to bring in more riders. Meanwhile the company rode careful herd on the bison, as the Sioux themselves had done, keeping them always within sight and contained by their mounted cordon. When reinforcements came this herd, led by the only master bull yet encountered, was transported intact to a safe preserve.

WHEN THERE was a real need or even a special desire among his people Stabs-The-Bear interceded endlessly with those in charge at the agency. Because he was helpful to all, the favors he asked were usually granted. Stabs-The-Bear had found, however, that a group request carried far more weight than the wishes of one or two. Thus it was that at a gathering of elders in the lodge of Horned Thunder one day, he dropped the suggestion that it would greatly hearten the people to have a few buffalo somewhere about. The mere knowledge that their totem was near them would lift their hearts upward, he said, and he had heard that there were buffalo less than two hundred miles away. This was a small herd protected by the White Father at Washington and some of them might be brought here.

There were *hau's* of approval as in the councils of old, and it was decided that they go in a body and make the request to the commandant, with Stabs-The-Bear acting as their spokesman. Standing Elk was not of this number for he was ill again and could not leave his tipi. Even when told of the plan and of the commandant's willingness to pass along the request, the old *shaman* did not believe in it. The buffalo were gone, he said. Even if this were not so white men would never keep such a promise.

When a moon or two had passed without result Standing Elk was doubly sure of this. But Stabs-The-Bear understood that such things took time, and explained to his foster father that Government itself had to be informed of the plan and consent to it before the buffalo could be moved. He knew the hunger in Standing Elk's heart for some contact with *Wahkan-Tanka*, and the Sioux way to this was communion with the herd spirit. The mere sight of some buffalo would renew the *shaman's* faith, Stabs-The-Bear felt sure. So he kept pressing the matter with the commandant until the plan was actually in motion.

On an autumn morning word came that the buffalo the Oglala elders had asked for had finally been driven to a point within forty miles of the agency and a new preserve established there. Stabs-The-Bear went to the commandant with still another request: that the *shaman*, his father, might ride out with him, so the two could see the buffalo and report to their people. The commandant gave permission.

Stabs-The-Bear found Standing Elk in his tipi by the small central fire, with Chief Horned Thunder sitting opposite. Respectfully the young *shaman* joined them in their quiet. There was a feeling in the air of long and fruitful silence about to terminate. No doubt the old *shaman* had been praying and making mystery that morning and the chief had been drawn to join him. Horned Thunder spoke out of the long silence.

"It is good medicine that one has had a vision after so long a time."

The *shaman's* head dipped once. "And in this place," he added.

"Truly one is glad to share the vision, Grandfather," said the old chief. "It is like the times when the herd was near and you rode forth to make peace with the buffalo before the fall hunt."

The *shaman* smoked for a space before replying. "The journey that I took in my dream was a long one. But there were buffalo, many buffalo at the end of it!"

Stabs-The-Bear spoke now: "But the journey is not too long, my father. The place is but two sleeps distant and there are buffalo at the end of it!"

The *shaman's* glance through the pipesmoke was sharp. "You, too, have been dreaming, my son!"

"No dream!" Stabs-The-Bear said. "You saw a true thing in your visions, my father, as always. There are buffalo, a small herd, two days ride from this place. And we have permission to go there!"

E V E N   A F T E R the start of the journey there seemed doubt at times in the old *shaman's* mind. But the sun and the wind of the open was happiness in itself after long confinement, and the October day was clear, the wind keen-edged. Hunting weather. The *shaman* sang often as he rode and on their frequent stops for rest he would take out his medicine bundle. To these periods of prayer the young *shaman* lent power and Standing Elk rose refreshed. Stabs-The-Bear knew the physical toll that the long ride was taking, but clearly his father's spirit was rising. Beneath the blanket the *shaman's* lean back was straighter than it had been in many moons and in the black eyes was a light of hope and renewal.

By the time they had stopped for their first sleep in the open and Stabs-The-Bear was cooking at their supper fire, Standing Elk had begun the old game chant. He ate little of the food his son laid out, nor would he try to sleep. Even when the late moon arched above the hills Standing Elk sat on before the small fire, chanting and praying and working with the sacred articles. In all of this Stabs-The-Bear was with him. The night fire under the stars and the tingle of the fall air on their faces was freedom itself. A great longing grew upon the younger man for them to ride on together and never return to the agency. The old *shaman* seemed to sense this for he turned to Stabs-The-Bear.

"His people come first in the heart of the true *shaman,* and this you are, my son. When they are held captive as our people are, cut off from the old strengths, then must the true *shaman* be strongest. In that new place you have been strong, my son."

"You are the strong one, my father," Stabs-The-Bear said. "Only now in my heart we were riding on and on together, beyond returning."

"It was the weakness of a moment," the *shaman* said, and waited. As Stabs-The-Bear remained silent he added, "One wishes to hear the strong words spoken, my son."

"I have waited only to find them, my father. They are your own words: 'His people come first in the heart of the true *shaman*.' The people are his heart. He has no other."

A F T E R A short sleep Standing Elk was up before the sun and pressing on, so that Stabs-The-Bear could but mount and follow. The pace was much faster than the day before, the old *shaman* in the lead. Now his hand was certain on the reins, for his old power of buffalo bringer and finder was upon him once more. As the sun climbed higher Stabs-The-Bear would have had his father stop for rest and food, but he would not.

Not even when the sun was at its highest would the old *shaman* pause. They had traveled so steadily and fast that the end of the journey was not far. Standing Elk sensed this. The urge forward which had driven him far beyond his bodily strength was slackening now, and he knew how tired he was, but it did not matter.

He was still riding ahead, his horse climbing a long, gradual slope. Once he caught himself with a jerk and gripped his horse's mane. Had he slept for an instant? No matter, he had the power for this trail. He began to chant once more to rouse himself, his voice rising to the limit of its power that the Great One might hear and lead him true.

No herd was yet in sight, but that now, that dark shape on top of a distant knoll, was surely a guardian bull. It was still a long way to go, but belief strengthened in him with every breath he drew. Without it he might not have been able to go on at all, for in truth he was very, very tired. Gradually it was breaking over him that it was no mere guardian bull that stood upon the knoll, and no wonder that there was no herd to be seen beyond, for this mighty one in himself represented all buffalo. Surely this was the Buffalo God who sometimes walked abroad and spoke to men.

Now the *shaman* heard a voice. He could not quite grasp the words but it seemed that he had still farther to ride this day. A burst of purest joy was in his breast, he lifted his hand, palm out.

"Wahkan-Tanka!"

In his reverence he had dismounted, or perhaps he

had fallen from the saddle. But it was better to be here on the ground, with the Great One about to speak again . . .

THROUGH HIS shaggy frontlet Kahtanka had watched the two mounted figures approaching. The riders were unarmed—Kahtanka had long since come to know that difference. Nor was there any threat in the feel of these men. Not even his two guardian cowbirds took alarm. It was long now since any man had brought danger to him, or to his small following; none at all since coming to this place among the hills. Kahtanka did not move.

One of the riders was on the ground now and quite still. The other came quickly forward to kneel beside him. Kahtanka continued to gaze at them and the horses standing quietly by. Then the one man lifted the other across his horse, and, leading the second horse, rode slowly back the way they had come.

After long brooding Kahtanka lowered his great head and resumed his feeding.